GETTING THE GIRL

Also by Markus Zusak:

The Underdog
Fighting Ruben Wolfe

The Book Thief

GETTING THE GIRL

MARKUS ZUSAK

Definitions

GETTING THE GIRL
A DEFINITIONS BOOK 978 1 849 41839 3

Originally published in Australia as WHEN DOGS CRY in 2001 by Pan Books,
an imprint of Pan Macmillan Australia.

First published in the United States as GETTING THE GIRL in 2003
by Arthur A. Levine Books, an imprint of Scholastic Press.

Published in Great Britain in 2013 by Definitions,
an imprint of Random House Children's Publishers UK
A Random House Group Company

1 3 5 7 9 10 8 6 4 2

Set in Perpetua

Definitions are published by Random House Children's Publishers UK,
61–63 Uxbridge Road, London W5 5SA

www.**randomhousechildrens**.co.uk
www.**totallyrandombooks**.co.uk
www.**randomhouse**.co.uk

Addresses for companies within The Random House Group Limited can be found at:
www.randomhouse.co.uk/offices.htm

THE RANDOM HOUSE GROUP Limited Reg. No. 954009

A CIP catalogue record for this book is available from the British Library.

Printed and bound by CPI Group (UK) Ltd, Croydon, CR0 4YY

For Scout

and

for Mum and Dad

1

It was Rube's girl's idea to make the beer ice-blocks not mine.

Let's start with that.

It just happened to be me who lost out because of it.

See, I'd always thought that at some point I'd grow up, but it hadn't happened yet. It's just the way it was.

In all honesty, I'd wondered if there would ever come a time when Cameron Wolfe (that's me) would pull himself together. I'd seen glimpses of a different me. It was a different me because in those increments of time I thought I actually became a winner.

The truth, however, was painful.

It was a truth that told me with a scratching internal brutality that I was me, and that winning wasn't natural for me. It had to be fought for, in the echoes and trodden footprints of my mind. In a way, I had to scavenge for moment of all-rightness.

I touched myself.

A bit.

OK.

OK.

A lot.

(There are people who've told me you shouldn't admit that sort of thing too early, on account of the fact that people might get offended. Well, all I can say to that is why the hell not? Why not tell the truth? Otherwise there's no bloody point really, is there?

Is there?)

It was just that I wanted to be touched by a girl someday. I wanted her to not look at me as if I was the filthy, torn, half-smiling, half-scowling underdog who was trying to impress her.

Her fingers.

In my mind, they were always soft, falling down my chest to my stomach. Her nails would be on my legs, just nice, handing shivers to my skin. I imagined it all the time, but refused to believe it was purely a matter of lust. The reason I can say this is that in my daydreams, the hands of the girl would always end up at my heart. Every time. I told myself that *that's* where I wanted her to touch me.

There was sex, of course.

Nakedness.

Wall to wall, in and out of my thoughts.

But when it was over it was her whispering voice I craved, and a human curled up in my arms. For me, though, it just wasn't a mouthful of reality. I was swallowing visions, and wallowing in my own mind, and feeling like I could happily drown inside a woman.

God, I wanted to.

I wanted to drown inside a woman in the feeling and drooling of the love I could give her. I wanted her pulse to crush me with its intensity. That's what I wanted. That's what I wanted myself to be.

Yet.

I wasn't.

The only mouthfuls I got were a glance here or there, and my own scattered hopes and visions.

The beer ice-blocks.

Of course.

I knew I was forgetting something.

It had been a warm day for winter, though the wind was still cold. The sun was warm, and kind of throbbing.

We were sitting in the back yard, listening to the

Sunday afternoon football coverage, and quite frankly, I was looking at the legs, hips, face and breasts of my brother's latest girlfriend.

The brother in question is Rube (Ruben Wolfe), and in the winter I'm talking about, he seemed to have a new girlfriend every few weeks or so. I could hear them sometimes when they were in our room – a call or shout or moan or even a whisper of ecstasy. I liked the latest girl from the start, I remember. Her name was nice. Octavia. She was a street performer, and also a nice person, compared with some of the scrubbers Rube had brought home.

We first met her down at the harbour one Saturday afternoon in late autumn. She was playing a harmonica so people would throw money into an old jacket that was sprawled out at her feet. There was a lot of money in it, and Rube and I watched her because she was damn good and could really make that harmonica howl. People would stand around sometimes and clap when she was done. Even Rube and I threw money in at one point, just after an old bloke with a walking stick and just before some Japanese tourists.

Rube looked at her.

She looked at him.

4

That was usually all it took, because that was Rube. My brother never really had to say or do anything. He just had to stand somewhere or scratch himself or even trip up a gutter and a girl would like him. It was just the way it was, and it was that way with Octavia.

'So where y' livin' these days?' Rube had asked her.

I remember the ocean green of her eyes rising then. 'Down south, in Hurstville.' He had her then already. I could tell 'You?'

And Rube had turned and pointed. 'You know those crappy streets past Central Station?'

She nodded.

'Well, that's us.' Only Rube could make those crappy streets sound like the best place on earth and with those words, Rube and Octavia had begun.

One of the best things about her was that she actually acknowledged my existence. She didn't look at me as if I was an obstacle stuck between her and Rube. She would always say, 'How's it goin', Cam?'

The truth is.

Rube never loved any of them.

He never cared about them.

He just wanted each one because she was next,

and why not take the next thing if it was better than the last?

Needless to say, Rube and I aren't too much alike when it comes to women.

Still.

I'd always liked that Octavia.

I liked it when we went inside that day and opened the fridge to see three-day-old soup, a carrot, a green thing, and one VB beer can sitting inside, All three of us bent down and stared.

'Perfect.'

It was Rube who said it, sarcastically.

'What *is* that?' Octavia asked.

'What?'

'That green thing.'

'I wouldn't have a clue.'

'An avocado?'

'Too big,' I said.

'What the hell *is* it?' Octavia asked again.

'Who cares?' Rube butted in. He had his eye on the VB. Its label was the only green thing he was staring at.

'That's Dad's,' I told him, still looking into the fridge. None of us moved.

'So?'

'So he went with Mum and Sarah to watch Steve's football game. He might want it when he comes home.'

'Yeah, but he might also buy some on the way.'

Octavia's breast brushed my shoulder when she turned and walked away. It felt so nice, it made me quiver.

Immediately, Rube reached in and grabbed the beer. 'It's worth a shot,' he stated. 'The old man's in a good mood these days anyway.'

He was right.

This time last year he was pretty miserable on account of having no work. This year he had plenty of work, and when he asked me to help on the odd Saturday or two, I helped him. So did Rube. My father's a plumber.

Each of us sat at the kitchen table.

Rube.

Octavia.

Me.

And the beer, sitting in the middle of the table, sweating.

'Well?'

Rube asked it.

'Well what?'

'Well what the hell are we gonna do with this beer, you stupid bastard.'

'Settle down, will y'.'

We smiled wryly.

Even Octavia smiled, because she'd grown used to the way Rube and I spoke to each other, or at least, the way Rube spoke to me.

'Do we split it three ways?' Rube continued. 'Or just pass it round.'

That was when Octavia had her great idea.

'How 'bout we make it into ice-blocks?'

'Is that some kind of sick joke?' Rube asked her.

'Of course not.'

'Beer ice-blocks?' Rube shrugged and considered it. 'Well, I s'pose. It's warm enough, ay. Have we got any of those plastic ice-block things? You know, with the stick?'

Octavia was already in the cupboards, and she found what she was after. 'Pay dirt,' she grinned (and she had a lovely mouth, with straight, white, sexy teeth).

'Right.'

This was serious now.

Rube opened the beer and was about to pour it out, in equal amounts, of course.

Interruption.

Me.

'Shouldn't we wash 'em or somethin'?'

'Why?'

'Well they've prob'ly been in that cupboard for ten years.'

'So what?'

'So they're probably all mouldy and mangy, and—'

'Can I just pour the goddamn beer!?'

We all laughed again, through the tension, and finally, painstakingly, Rube poured three equal portions of beer into the ice-block containers. He fixed the stick on each of them so they were straight down.

'Right,' he said. 'Thank Christ for that,' and he walked slowly to the fridge.

'In the freezer bit,' I told him.

He stopped, mid-walk, turned slowly and carefully back round, and said, 'Do you seriously think I'm pathetic enough to put beer which I just took *from* the fridge and poured into *ice*-blocks back in just the fridge?'

'Y' never know.'

He turned away again and kept walking. 'Octavia, open the freezer, will y'.'

She did it.

'Thanks, love.'

'No worries.'

Then it was just a matter of waiting for them to set.

We sat around in the kitchen for a while, until Octavia spoke, to Rube.

'You feel like doin' something?' she asked him. With most girls, that was my cue to leave. Octavia, though, I wasn't sure. I just cleared out anyway.

'Where y' going?' Rube asked me.

'Not sure.'

I went out of the kitchen, took my jacket for later, and walked onto the front porch. Half out the door, I mentioned, 'Maybe down the dog track. Maybe just out wanderin'.'

'Fair enough.'

'See y' later, Cam.'

With a last look at Rube and a glance at Octavia, I could see desire in each of the eyes I met. Octavia had desire for Rube. Rube just had desire for a girl. Pretty simple, really.

'See y's later,' I said, and walked out.

The flyscreen door slammed behind me.

My feet dragged.

I reached each arm into the jacket.

Warm sleeves.

Crumpled collar.

Hands in pockets.

OK.

I walked.

Soon evening worked its way into the sky, and the city hunched itself down. I knew where I was going. Without knowing, without thinking, I knew. I was going to a girl's place. It was a girl I had met last year at the dog track.

She liked.

She liked.

Not me.

She liked Rube.

She'd even called me a loser once when she was talking to him, and I'd listened in as my brother smacked her down with words and shoved her away.

What I'd been doing lately was standing outside her house, across the road. I stood and stared and watched and hoped. And I left, after the curtains were drawn for a while. Her name was Stephanie.

That night, which I think of now as the beer ice-block night, I stood and stared a bit longer than usual. I stood and imagined walking home with her and opening the door for her. I imagined it hard, till a reaching pain pulled me inside out.

I stood.

Soul on the outside.

Flesh within.

'Ah well.'

It was a fair walk because she lived in Glebe and I lived closer to Central, on a small street with ragged gutters and the train line just beyond. I was used to it, though – both the distance and the street. In a way, I'm actually proud of where I come from. The small house. The craggy road. The Wolfe family.

Many minutes shuffled forward as I walked home, and when I saw my dad's panel van on our street, I even smiled.

Things had actually been OK for everyone lately.

Steve, my other brother.

Sarah, my sister.

Mrs Wolfe – the resilient Mrs Wolfe, my mother, who cleans houses and at the hospital for a living.

Rube.

Dad.

And me.

For some reason that night when I walked home, I felt peaceful. I felt happy for all of my family, because things really did seem to be going OK for them. All of them.

A train rushed past, and I felt like I could hear the whole city in it.

It came to me and then glided away.

Things always seem to glide away.

They come to you, stay a moment, then leave again.

That train seemed like a friend that day, and when it was gone, I felt like something in me tripped. I was alone on the street, and although I was still peaceful, the brief happiness left and a sadness tore me open very slowly and deliberately. City lights shone across the air, reaching their arms out to me, but I knew they'd never quite make it.

I composed myself and made my way onto the front porch. Inside they were talking about the ice-blocks and the missing beer. I was actually looking forward to eating my share of it, even though I can never finish a full can or bottle of beer. (I just stop being thirsty, to which Rube once said, 'So do I, mate, but I still keep drinkin' it.') In this case, the ice-block idea was at least halfway interesting, so I was ready to go in and give it a shot.

'I was planning on drinking that beer when we got home.'

I could hear my father talking just before I went inside. There was an element of bastardry in his voice as he continued. 'And whose brilliant idea was it to make ice-blocks out of *my* beer, sorry, my *last* beer, anyway? Who was it?'

There was a pause.

A long one.

Silent.

Then, finally, 'Mine,' came the answer, just as I walked into the house.

The only question is, who said it?

Was it Rube?

Octavia?

No.

It was me.

Don't ask me why, but I just didn't want Octavia to cop a bit of a battering (verbally, of course) from Clifford Wolfe, my father. The odds were that he'd be all nice to her about it, but still, it wasn't worth the risk. Much better for him to think it was me. He was used to me doing ridiculous things.

'Why aren't I surprised?' he asked, turning to face me. He was holding the ice-blocks in question in his hands.

He smiled.

A good thing, trust me.

Then he laughed and said, 'Well, Cameron, you won't mind if I eat yours then, will y'?'

'Of course not.' You always say 'of course not' in that situation because you figure out pretty quick that your old man's really asking, 'Will I take the ice-block or will I make you suffer in a hundred different other ways?' Naturally, you play it safe.

The ice-blocks were handed out, and a small smile was exchanged between Octavia and me, then Rube and me.

Rube held his ice-block out to me. 'Bite?' he asked, but I declined.

I left the room, hearing my father say, 'Pretty good, actually.'

The bastard.

'Where'd y' go before?' Rube asked me later in our room, after Octavia had left. Each of us lay on our bed, talking across the room.

'Just around a bit.'

'Down Glebe way?'

I looked over. 'What's that mean?'

'It means,' Rube sighed, 'that Octavia and I followed you once, just out of interest. We saw y' outside a house, starin' into the window. You're a bit of a lonely bastard, aren't y'?'

Moments twisted and curled then, and off in the distance I could hear traffic, roaring almost silently. Far from all this. Far from Cameron and Ruben Wolfe discussing what in the hell I was doing outside the house of a girl who cared nothing for me.

I swallowed, breathed in, and answered my brother.

'Yeah,' I said. 'I guess I am.'

There was nothing else I could say. Nothing to cover it up. There was only a slight moment of waiting, truth and feeling, then a crack, and I said more. It's that Stephanie girl.'

'The bitch,' Rube spat.

'I know but—'

'I know,' Rube interrupted. 'It makes no difference if she said she hated you or called you a loser. Y' feel what y' feel.'

Y' feel what y' feel.

It was one of the truest things Rube had ever said, just before a quietness smothered the room.

From next-door's back yard we could hear a dog barking. It was Miffy, the pitiful Pomeranian we loved to hate, but still walked a few times a week anyway.

'Sounds like Miffy's a bit upset,' Rube said after a while.

'Yeah,' and I laughed a bit.

A bit of a lonely bastard. A bit of a lonely bastard.

Rube's statement reverberated inside me till his voice was like a hammer.

Later, when I got up and sat on the front porch and watched shadows of traffic filter past, I told myself it was OK to be like this, as long as I stayed hungry. It felt like something was arriving in me. It was something I couldn't see or know or understand. It was just there, mingling into my blood.

Very quickly, very suddenly, words fell through my mind. They landed on the floor of my thoughts, and in there, down there, I started to pick the words up. They were excerpts of truth gathered from inside me.

Even in the night, in bed, they woke me.

They painted themselves onto the ceiling.

They burned themselves onto the sheets of memory laid out in my mind.

When I woke up the next day, I wrote the words down, on a torn-up piece of paper. And to me, the world changed colour that morning.

WORDS OF CAMERON

The city streets are lined with truth, and I walk through them. Sometimes, they walk through me. Thoughts are like blood sometimes, when I think of women and sex and everything in between. I collect my thoughts as if they will stain me, murder me, and then resurrect me.

I've stopped sometimes and felt the world turning, and I think there are hands that turn it.

I guess I think we turn the world ourselves, often making our hands and fingers dirty, and our wrists sore, from the work.

I feel like the world is a factory.

It's the factory of God's light and we just work here.

I clock onto the truth — that I'm small in terms of this world, but I'm awake.

Days and nights fight each other. The hours and minutes are the bruises, and as each day passes by, I know that I'm alone.

They say that no one really likes being alone, and I know that I am one of them. Having said that, I think there's something tough in it. Something stoic and strong and uncensored.

Another truth is that I am an animal.

A human animal.

With feral thoughts, and ragged furry hair that reached to the sky.

God, how I want the skin of women! I want it on my lips and hands and fingers. How I want to taste her . . .

But then — then —

Beneath that.

That's not enough!

Yes, when that's done, I also want the everything that's her to fill up so much in front of me that it spills and shivers and gives, just like I'm prepared to do myself.

But for now, happiness throws stones.

It guards itself.

I wait.

2

My oldest brother Steven Wolfe is what you'd call a hard bastard. He's successful. He's smart. He's determined.

The thing with Steve is that nothing will ever stop him. It's not only *in* him. It's on him, around him. You can smell it, sense it. His voice is hard and measured, and everything about him says, 'You're not going to get in my way.' When he talks to people, he's friendly enough, but the minute they try one on him, forget it. If someone tries to trample him, you'd put your house on it that he'll do twice the job on them. Steve never forgets.

Me on the other hand.

I'm not really like Steve in that way.

I kind of wander around a lot.

That's what I do.

Personally, I think it comes from not having many friends, or in fact, any friends at all, really.

There was a time when I really ached to be part

of a pack of friends. I wanted a bunch of guys I'd be prepared to bleed for. It never happened. When I was younger I had a mate called Greg and he was an OK guy. Actually, we did a lot together. Then we drifted apart. It happens to people all the time, I guess. No big deal. In a way, I'm part of the Wolfe pack, and that's enough. I know without doubt that I'd bleed for anyone in my family.

Anyplace.

Anytime.

My best mate is Rube.

Steve, on the other hand, has plenty of friends, but he wouldn't bleed for any of them, because he wouldn't trust them to bleed for him. In that way he's just as alone as me.

He's alone.

I'm alone.

There just happen to be people around him, that's all. (People meaning friends, of course.)

Anyway, the point of telling you about all this is that sometimes when I go out wandering at night I'll go up to Steve's apartment, which is about a kilometre from home. It's usually when I can't handle standing outside that girl's house, when the ache of it aches too much.

He's got a nice place, Steve, on the second floor, and he has a girl who lives there as well. Often she's not there because she works in a company that sends her on business trips and all that kind of thing. I always thought she was pretty nice, I s'pose, since she tolerated me when I went up to visit. Her name's Sal and she's got nice legs. That's a fact I can never escape.

'Hey, Cam.'

'Hey, Steve.'

That's what we say every time I go up and he's home.

It was no different the night after the beer iceblock incident. I buzzed from downstairs. He called me up. We said what we always say.

The funny thing is that over time, we've become at least slightly better at talking to each other. The first time, we sat there and had black coffee and said nothing. We each just let our eyes swirl into the pools of coffee and let our voices be numb and silent. There was always a thought in me that maybe Steve held a sort of grudge against everyone in the Wolfe family because he seemed to be the only winner, in the world's eyes, anyway. It was like he might have good cause to be ashamed of us, I was never sure.

In recent times, since Steve decided to play one

22

more year of football, we'd even gone to the local ground and kicked the ball around. (Or in truth, Steve had practice shots at goal and I returned them.) We'd go there and he'd turn the lights on, and even if it was extra cold and the earth was coated with frost and our lungs were trodden with winter air, we always stayed for quite a while. If it got too late, he even dropped me home.

He never asked how anyone was. Never. Steve was more specific.

'Is Mum still workin' herself into the ground?'

'Yeah.'

'Dad got plenty of work?'

'Yeah.'

'Sarah still goin' out, getting smashed, and comin' home reeking of club and smoke and cocktails?'

'Nah, she's off that now. Always workin' overtime shifts. She's OK.'

'Rube still Mr Excitement? One girl after another? One fight after another?'

'Nah, there's no one game enough to fight him any more.' Rube is without doubt one of the best fighters in this part of the city. He's proved it. Countless times. 'You're right about the girls, though,' I continued.

'Of course.' He nodded and that's when things always get a little edgy – when it comes to the question of me.

What could he possibly ask?

'Still got no mates, Cameron?'

'Still completely alone, Cameron?'

'Still wanderin' the streets?'

'Still got your hands at work under the sheets?'

No.

Every time, he avoids it, just like the night I'm talking about.

He asked, 'And you?' A breath. 'Survivin'?'

'Yeah.' I nodded. 'Always.'

After that there was more silence, till I asked him who he was playing against this weekend.

As I told you earlier, Steve decided to have one last year of football. At the start of the season, he was begged to go back by his old team. They begged hard, and finally, he gave in, and they haven't lost a game yet. That was Steve.

That Monday night, I still had my words in my pocket, because I'd decided to carry them every-where with me. They were still on that creased piece of paper, and often I would check that they were still there. For a moment, at Steve's table, I imagined myself telling him about it. I heard myself explaining how it made me feel like I was worth it, like I was just *OK*. But I said nothing. Absolutely nothing, even as I thought, *I guess that's what we all crave once in a while, OKness. All-rightness*. It was a vision of looking inside a mirror and not wanting, not needing, because everything was there.

With the words in my hands, that was how I felt.

I nodded.

At the prospect of it.

'What?' Steve asked me.

'Nothing.'

'Fair enough.'

The phone rang.

Steve: 'Hello.'

The other end: 'Yeah, it's me.'

'Who the hell's *me?*'

It was Rube.

Steve knew it.

I knew it.

Even though I was a good distance from the phone, I could tell it was Rube, because he talks loud, especially on the phone.

'Is Cameron there?'

'Yeah.'

'Are y's going up the oval?'

'Maybe,' at which point Steve looked over and I nodded. 'Yes, we are,' he answered.

'I'll be up there in ten minutes.'

'Right. Bye.'

'Bye.'

Secretly, I think I preferred it when it was only Steve and me who went. Rube was always brilliant, always starting something and mucking around, but with Steve and me, I enjoyed the quiet intensity of it. We might never have said a word – and I might have only kicked the ball back hard and straight, and let the dirt and smell of it thump onto my chest – but I loved the feeling of it, and the idea that I was part of something unspoken and true.

Not that I never had moments like that with Rube. I had plenty of great moments with Rube. I guess it's just that with Steve, you really have to earn things like that. You'd wait for ever if you wanted one for free. Like I've said before, for other reasons, that's Steve.

On the way down to the ground floor a few minutes later, he said, 'I'm sore as hell from yesterday's game. I got belted in the ribs about five times.'

At Steve's games it was always the same. The other team always made sure he hit the ground especially hard. He always got up.

We stood on the street, waiting for Rube.

'Hey boys.'

When he arrived, Rube was puffing gently from the run. His thick, curly, furry hair was too attractive for its own good, even though it was a lot shorter than it used to be. He was wearing only a jersey, sawn-off track pants, and gymmies. Smoke came from his mouth from the cold.

We started walking, and Steve was his usual self. He wore the same pair of old jeans he always did at the oval and a flanno shirt. Athletic shoes. His eyes took aim, scanning the path, and his hair was short and wiry and tough-looking. He was tall and abrupt and exactly the kind of guy you wanted to be walking the streets with.

Especially in the city.

Especially in the dark.

Then there was me.

Maybe the best way to describe me that night was by looking again at my brothers. Both of them were in control. Rube, in a reckless, *no matter what happens, I'll be ready when it comes* kind of way. Steve, in a *there's nothing you can do that's going to hurt me* way.

My own face focused on many things, but never for too long, remaining eventually on my feet, as they travelled across the slightly slanted road. My hair was sticking up. It was curly and ruffled. I wore the same jersey as Rube (only mine was slightly more faded), old jeans, my spray jacket and boots. I told myself that although I could never look the same as my brothers, I still had *something*.

I had the words in my pocket.

Maybe that was what I had.

That, and knowing that I've walked the city a thousand times on my own and that I could walk these streets with more feeling than anyone, as if I was walking through myself. I'm pretty sure that was what it was – more a feeling than a look.

At the oval Steve had shots at goal.

Rube had shots at goal.

I sent the ball back to them.

When Steve had a shot, the ball rose up high and kept climbing between the posts. It was clean, ranging, and when it came down, it rushed onto my chest with a complete, numbing force. Rube's ball, on the other hand, spun and spiralled, low and charging, but also went through the posts each time.

They kicked them from everywhere. In front. Far out. Even past the edges of the field.

'Hey Cam!' Rube yelled at one point. 'Come out and have a shot!'

'Nah, mate, I'll be right.'

They made me, though. Twenty metres out, twenty metres to the left. I moved in with my heart shuddering. My feet stepped in, I kicked it, and the ball reached for the posts.

It curved.

Spun.

Then it collided with the right-hand post and slumped to the grass.

Silence.

Steve mentioned, 'It was a good shot, Cameron,' and the three of us stood there, in the wet, weeping grass.

It was quarter past eight then.

At eight-thirty, Rube left, and I'd had another seven shots.

At just past nine-thirty, Steve was still standing behind the posts, and I still hadn't got it through. Clumps of darkness grew heavier in the sky, and it was just Steve and me.

Each time my brother sent the ball back, I

searched for a note of complaint in him, but it never came. When we were younger he might have called me useless. Hopeless. All he did that night, however, was kick the ball back and wait again.

When the ball finally fought its way up and fell through the posts, Steve caught it and stood there.

No smile.

No nod of the head, or any recognition.

Not yet.

Soon he walked with the ball under his arm, and when he was perhaps ten metres short of me, he gave me a certain look.

His eyes looked differently at me.

His expression was swollen.

Then.

I've never seen a person's face shatter like his did.

With pride.

HUNGER AND DESIRE ON A FRONT PORCH NIGHT

Tonight, I sit on the front porch as I write these words. The wind crawls up my sleeves and the pen wavers in my hand.

The city is cold and dark.

The streets are filled with numbness and the sky is sinking. Dark, dark sky.

Beside me, I look at the memory of twenty out and twenty left of the posts. I see a shattering face and the verge of something to become.

I tell me:

Let these words be footsteps, because I have a long way to travel. Let the words walk the dirty streets. Let them make their way across the crying grass. Let them stand and breathe and pant smoke in winter evenings. And when they're tired and have fallen down, let them buckle to their feet and arc around me, watchful.

I want these words to be actions.

Give them flesh and bones, I say to me, and eyes of hunger and desire, so they can write and fight me through the night.

3

Faggot. Poofter. Wanker.

These are common words in my neighbourhood when someone wants to *give you some*, tell you off, or just plain humiliate you. They'll also call you one of those things if you show some sign that you're in some way different from the regular, run-of-the-mill sort of guy who lives in this part of the city. You might also get it if you've annoyed someone in some inadvertent way and the person has nothing better to say. For all I know it's the same everywhere, but I can't really speak for anywhere else. The only place I know is this.

This city.

These streets.

Soon you'll know why I've mentioned it . . .

On Thursday that week I decided I should go and get a haircut, which is always a pretty dangerous decision, especially when your hair sticks up as stubborn and chronic as mine. You just have to pray that it won't end in tragedy. You hope beyond all hope that the barber won't ignore all instructions and butcher your head to pieces. But it's a risk you have to take.

'Har-low, mate,' the barber said when I entered the shop, deeper into the city. 'Have a seat, I won't be long.'

In the scungy waiting area there was quite a good range of magazines, though you could tell each one had been sitting there for the last few years, judging by the dates of issue. There was *Time*, *Rolling Stone*, some fishing thing. *Who Weekly*, some computer thing, *Black and White*, *Surfing Life* and, always a favourite, *Inside Sport*. Of course the best thing about the *Inside Sport* magazine is not the sport, but the scantily clad woman who is planted on the cover. She is always firm and has desire in her eyes. Her swimsuit is nice and open, her legs long and tanned and elegant. She has breasts you can only imagine your hands touching and massaging. (Sorry, but it's true.) She has hips of extreme grace, a golden, flat stomach, and a neck you can only imagine yourself sucking on. Her lips are always full and hungry. The eyes say, 'Take me.'

You remind yourself that there are some pretty

good articles in *Inside Sport*, but you know you're lying. Of course there *are* some good articles in the magazine, but that sure as hell isn't what makes you pick it up. It's always the woman. Always. Trust me on this one.

So, typically, I surveyed the area and made sure no one was looking when I picked up the *Inside Sport* magazine, opened it quickly, and pretended to scan the contents page for any good articles. I was (predictably) seeing which page the woman was on.

Seventy-six.

'OK, mate,' the barber said.

'Me?'

'There's no one else waiting, is there?'

Yeah, but, I thought helplessly, *I haven't got to page seventy-six yet!*

It was futile.

The barber was ready, and if there's one man you don't keep waiting it's the guy about to cut your hair. He's all-powerful. In fact, he might as well be God. *That's* the kind of power he has. A few months at barber school and a man becomes the most important person in your life for ten or fifteen minutes. The golden rule: Don't give him a hard time or there'll be hell to pay.

Immediately, I threw the magazine back to the table, face-down so the barber wouldn't know right away what a pervert I am. He'd have to wait until later when he tidied the magazines.

Sitting in the chair (it sounds about as dangerous as the electric chair), I considered the whole woman on the cover situation.

'Short?' the barber asked me.

'Nah, not too short please, mate. I'm just tryin' to have it so it doesn't always stick up.'

'Easier said than done, ay?'

'Yeah.'

We exchanged a look of mutual friendliness and I felt much more at ease in the firing line of the scissors, the chair and the barber.

He started cutting and, like I said a minute ago, I reviewed the woman on the cover situation. My theory on this subject was and still is that I obviously desire the physicality of a woman. Yet, I honestly believe that *that* part of my desire for a girl is somewhere on the surface of my soul, whereas further and much deeper inside is the fiercer desire to please her, treat her right, and be immersed by the spirit of her.

I honestly believe that.

Honestly.

Still, I had to stop thinking about it and talk to the barber. That's another rule of the barbershop. If you talk to the man and get him to like you, maybe he won't screw it up. That's what you hope for anyway. It doesn't mean you'll have instant success, but it might help, so you try it. There are no guarantees in the world of barbershops. It's a gamble no matter which way you look at it. I had to start talking, and fast.

'So how's business?' I asked, as the barber cut his way through the thickness of my hair.

'Aah, you know, mate.' He stopped, and smiled at me in the mirror. 'Here 'n' there. Keepin' my head above water. That's the main thing.'

We talked for quite a while after that, and the barber told me how long he'd been working in the city and how much people have changed. I agreed with everything he said, with a dangerous nod of my head or a quiet 'Yeah, that sounds about right.' He was a pretty nice guy, to tell you the truth. Very big. Quite hairy. A husky voice.

I asked if he lived upstairs from the shop and he said, 'Yep, for the last twenty-five years.' That was when I pitied him a little, because I imagined him never going anywhere or doing anything. Just cutting hair. Eating a dinner alone. Maybe microwave dinners (though his dinners couldn't be much worse than the ones Mrs Wolfe cooked, God bless her).

'Do you mind me askin' if you ever got married?' I asked him.

'Of course I don't mind,' he answered. 'I had a wife but she died a few years ago. I go down the cemetery every weekend, but I don't put flowers down. I don't talk.' He sighed a bit and he was very sincere. Truly. 'I like to think I did enough of that when she was alive, you know?'

I nodded.

'It's no good once a person's dead. You gotta do it when you're together, still living.'

He'd stopped cutting for a few moments now, so I could continue nodding without risk. I asked, 'So what do you do when you're standin' there, at the grave?'

He smiled. 'I just remember, that's all.'

That's nice, I thought, but I didn't say it. I only smiled at the man behind me in the mirror. I had a vision of the large hairy man standing there at the cemetery, knowing that he gave everything he could. I also imagined myself there with him, on a dark grey day. Him in his white barber's coat. Me in the usual. Jeans. Flanno. Spray jacket.

'OK?' he turned and said to me in the vision.

'OK?' he said in the shop.

I woke back into reality and said, 'Yeah, thanks a lot, it's good,' even though I knew it would be standing up within forty-eight hours. I was happy, though, but not only for the haircut. The conversation too.

With my hair congregating around my feet, I paid twelve dollars and said, 'Thanks a lot. It was nice talking to you.'

'Same here,' and the large hairy barber smiled and I felt guilty about the magazine. I could only hope he would understand the different layers of my soul. After all, he was a barber. Barbers are supposed to have the answers to running the country, along with taxi drivers and obnoxious radio commentators. I thanked him again and said goodbye.

Once outside, it was still mid-afternoon, so *Why not?* I thought. *I might as well head over to Glebe.*

Needless to say, I got there and stood outside the girl's house.

Stephanie.

It was as good a place as any to watch the sun collapse behind the city, and after a while I sat down against a wall and thought again about the barber.

The importance of it was that he and I were really doing similar things, only in reverse order. He was remembering. I was anticipating. (Hopeful, almost ludicrous anticipation, I admit.)

Once it was dark, I decided I'd better get home for dinner. It was leftover steak, I think, with vegetables boiled into oblivion.

I got up.

I slipped my hands into my pockets.

Then I looked, hoped and walked, in that order.

Pathetic, I know, but it was my life, I guess. No point denying it.

It turned out to be later than I thought when I finally left, and I decided to get the bus back to my own neighbourhood.

At the bus stop there was a handful of people waiting. There was a man with a briefcase, a chain-smoking woman, a guy who looked like a labourer or carpenter, and a couple who leaned on each other and kissed a while as they waited.

I couldn't help it.

I watched.

Not obviously, of course. Just a quick look here and there.

Damn.

I got caught.

'What are *you* lookin' at?' The guy spat his words at me. 'Don't you have anything better to do?'

Nothing.

That was my reply.

Absolutely nothing.

'Well?'

Then the girl got stuck into me as well.

'Why don't y' go and stare at someone else, y' weirdo.' She had blonde hair, green eyes shrunken in under the streetlight, and a voice like a blunt knife. She beat me with it. 'Y' wanker.'

Typical.

You get called that name so many times around here, but this time it hurt. I guess it hurt because it was a girl. I don't know. In a way, it was kind of depressing that this was what we'd come to. We can't even wait for a bus in peace.

I know, I know. I should have barked back at them, nice and hard, but I didn't. I couldn't. Some Wolfe, ay. Some wild dog I turned out to be. All I did was steal one last look, to see if they were about to level some final fragments of abuse at me.

The guy was also blond. Not tall or short. He

wore dark trousers, boots, a black jacket and a sneer.

Meanwhile, the briefcase man checked his watch. The chain smoker lit up another. The labourer shifted his weight from one foot to the other.

Nothing more was said, but when the bus came, everyone pushed on and I was last.

'Sorry.'

When I got on and tried to pay, the driver told me that fares had just gone up and I didn't have enough money for a ticket.

I got off, smiled ruefully, and stood there.

The bus was pretty empty – the final insult.

As I started walking, I watched it pull away and shove itself along the street. Many thoughts staggered through me, including:

* How late I'd be for dinner.
* Whether or not anyone would ask where I'd been.
* Whether Dad wanted Rube and me to work with him on Saturday.
* If the girl named Stephanie would ever come out and see me (if she knew I was there at all).
* How much long it would take for Rube to get rid of Octavia.

* If Steve clung to the memory of the look we'd exchanged on Monday night as often as I did.
* How my sister Sarah was doing lately. (We hadn't spoken for a while.)
* Whether or not Mrs Wolfe was ever disappointed in me or knew that I had turned out such a lone figure.
* And how the barber was feeling above his shop.

I also realized as I walked, then began to run, that I didn't even have any bad feelings towards the couple who'd abused me. I knew I should have, but I didn't. Sometimes I think I need a bit more mongrel in me.

THE CEMETERY

There's a cemetery in my mind and I can see my own grave, on a blue-sky day with cotton clouds and angry sun.

People pass by that grave.

They speak and turn and wilt under the heat of the horizon and the scattered voice of death.

I can see fear churning in their hearts, as they build fences around what they say and believe, and what they tell the people around them. Only certain things make it out, onto the heated grass.

I write and hope – to stand in this vision long enough to see a shadow emerge over my grave.

No flowers.

No spoken words.

Only a person.

Remembering.

'This dog's an absolute embarrassment,' said Rube, and I knew that some things would never change. They would only slip away and return.

After the whole bus-stop issue, I got home, and after dinner, Rube and I were taking Miffy, our neighbour's midget dog, for his usual walk. As always, we wore our hoods over our heads so no one could recognize us, because in the words of Rube, the sight of Miffy was an absolute shocker.

'When Keith gets another dog,' he suggested, 'we'll tell him to get a Rottweiler. Or a Doberman. Or at least something we can be seen in public with.'

We stopped at an intersection.

Rube bent down to Miffy.

In an over-friendly voice, he said, 'Aren't you an ugly little bastard, Miffy, ay? Aren't you? Yes you are. You are, you know,' and the dog licked its lips and panted quite happily really. If only he had some idea that Rube was giving him a good mouthful. We crossed the street.

My feet dragged.

Rube's feet ambled.

Miffy pranced, and his chain jingled next to him, in time with his breathing.

Looking down at him, I realized he had the body of a rodent and the fur of something that can only be called stupendous. Like he'd gone a thousand rounds with a spin dryer. The probem was, we happened to love that dog, in spite of everything. Even that night, when we got home, I gave him the piece of steak Sarah couldn't finish at dinner. Unfortunately, it was a bit too tough to Miffy's pitiful little teeth and he nearly choked on it.

'Bloody hell, Cam,' Rube laughed. 'What are y' trying to do to the poor little bastard? He's gaggin' on it.'

'I thought it'd be all right.'

'All right, my arse. Look at him.' He pointed. 'Look at him!'

'What should I do, then?'

Rube had an idea. 'Maybe you oughta get it out of his mouth, chew it up a bit, and *then* give it to him.'

'What?' I looked at him. 'You want me to put *that* in my mouth?'

'That's right.'

'Maybe *you* should.'

'No way.'

So basically, we pretty much let Miffy choke a bit. In the end it didn't sound all that serious anyway.

'It'll build his character,' Rube suggested. 'Nothin' like a good choking to toughen a dog up.' We both watched intently as Miffy eventually finished off the steak.

When he was done and we were sure he hadn't choked himself to death, we took him home.

'We should just throw him over the fence,' Rube said, but we both knew we never would. There's a big difference between watching a dog half choke and throwing him over the fence. Besides, our neighbour Keith would be pretty unthrilled with us. He could be a bit unpleasant, Keith, especially when it came to that dog of his. You wouldn't think such a hard man would own such a fluffy kind of dog, but I'm sure he probably just blamed it on his wife.

'It's the wife's dog,' I can imagine him telling the boys at the pub. 'I'm just lucky I've got those two shit-head boys next door to walk him – their old lady makes 'em do it.' He could be a hard man, Keith, but OK nonetheless.

Speaking of hard men, it turned out that Dad did want our help on the upcoming Saturday. He pays us quite generously now, and he's always pretty happy. A while back, like I've said before, when he struggled to get work, he was pretty miserable, but these days it was good to work with him. Sometimes we went and got fish 'n' chips for lunch, and we played cards on top of Dad's small, dirty red cooler, but only as long as we all worked out guts out. Cliff Wolfe was a fan of working your guts out, and to be fair, so were Rube and I. We were also fans of fish 'n' chips and cards, even if it was usually the old man who won. Either he won or the game was taking too long and he cut it short. Some things can't be helped.

What I haven't mentioned is that Rube also had another job. He left school last year and got an apprenticeship with a builder, despite getting an abysmal result on his final exams.

I remember when he got them delivered.

He opened the envelope next to the slanted, slurred front gate of our house.

'How'd y' go?' I asked.

'Well, Cam.' He smiled, as if he was thoroughly pleased with himself. 'If I can sum it up in two

words. The first word is *completely*. The second word
is *shithouse*.'

And yet, he got a job.

Straight away.

Typical Rube.

He didn't need to work with the old man on
Saturdays, but for some reason, he did. Maybe it was
an act of respect. Dad asked, so Rube said yes. Maybe
he didn't want anyone to think he was lazy. I don't
know.

Either way, we were working with ol' Cliff that
weekend, and he woke us nice and early. It was still
dark.

We were waiting for Dad to get out of the bathroom (which he's always likely to leave in a pretty
horrendous state, smell-wise), when Rube and I
decided we'd get the cards out early.

As Rube dealt the cards at the kitchen table, I
recalled what happened a few weeks earlier, when we
had a game during breakfast. It wasn't a bad idea, but
I managed to spill my cornflakes all over the deck
because I was still half asleep. Even this week there
was still a dried cornflake glued to a card I threw
onto the out pile.

Rube picked it up.

Examined it.

'Huh.'

Me: 'I know.'

'You're pitiful.'

'I know.' I could only agree.

The toilet flushed, the water ran, and Dad came out of the bathroom.

'We go?'

We nodded and gathered up the cards.

At the job, Rube and I dug hard and talked and laughed. I'll admit that Rube's always good for a bit of a laugh. He was telling me a story about an old girlfriend of his who always munched on his ears.

'In the end I had to buy her some bloody chewie. Otherwise I wouldn't have my ears any more.'

Octavia, I thought.

I wondered what story he would have about her in a few weeks' time, when it was dead and gone and thrown out. Her searching eyes, ruffled hair, and human legs and nice feet. I wondered what quirks of hers he'd have to talk about. Maybe she insisted on him touching her leg in a movie, or liked turning her fingers in his hand. I didn't know.

It was quick.

I spoke.

'Rube?'

'What?'

He stopped digging and looked at me.

'How much longer for you and Octavia?'

'A week. Maybe two.'

There was nothing for me to do but continue digging then, and the day wandered past.

At lunch, the fish was greasy and great.

The chips were sprayed with salt and drenched in vinegar.

When we ate, Dad looked at the paper, Rube took the TV guide, and I started writing more words in my head. No more cards today.

That night, Mrs Wolfe asked me how everything was going at school, and I returned to my earlier thoughts that week of whether or not she'd had cause lately to be disappointed in me. I told her everything was all right. For a moment, I debated whether I should tell someone about the words I'd started writing down, but I couldn't. In a way, I felt ashamed, even though my writing was the one thing that whispered OKness in my ear. I didn't speak about it, to anyone.

We cleaned up together, before dinner's leftovers had a chance to get stagnant, and she told me about the book she was reading called *My Brother Jack*. She said it was about two brothers and how one of them rose up but still regretted the way he lived and the way he was.

'You'll rise up one day,' were her second-to-last words. 'But don't be too hard on yourself,' were her last.

When she left and I was standing alone in the kitchen, I saw that Mrs Wolfe was brilliant. Not smart-brilliant, or any particular kind of brilliant. Just brilliant, because she was herself and even the wrinkles around her ageing eyes were the shaded colour of kindness. That was what made her brilliant.

'Hey Cameron.' My sister Sarah came to me later on. 'You feel like goin' out to Steve's game tomorrow?'

'OK,' I replied. I had nothing better to do.

'Good.'

On Sunday, Steve would be playing his usual game of football, but at a different ground from the local, out more Maroubra way. It was only Sarah and me who went to watch. We went up to his apartment and he drove us out there.

Something big happened at that game.

THE COLOUR OF KINDNESS

I've thought once in a while about the colour of kindness, and I realize that its shades and contrasts are not painted onto a person. They're worn in.

Have you ever stood in your kitchen and felt like falling to your knees?

I don't know.

There are very few things that I know for sure.

I know that when I eat fish and chips, my fingers and throat get greasy. The gorgeous ugliness of it slithers to my stomach, but it's all forgiven when my old man smiles at me, and I wouldn't trade that grease for anything.

When I look in the mirror, I see the colour of awkwardness and uncertainty and longing.

If there was an expert amongst these pages, they'd say that I just want to belong somewhere.

But the truth is, I'm not sure I want to belong.

Not like everyone else.

That's what scares me.

5

On the way up to Steve's, I wondered what the hell my sister Sarah was going to do with her life. She walked next to me, and most men who walked past us watched her. Many of them turned round once they'd gone past and took a second look at her body. It seemed that to them, that's all she was. The thought of it made me a little sick (not that I can talk), and I hoped she would never end up actually being that life.

'Friggin' perverts,' she said.

Which gave me hope.

The thing is, I think we're all perverts. All men. All women. All disgruntled little bastards like me. It's funny to think of my father as a pervert, or my mother. But somewhere, in the crevices of their souls, I'm sure they've slipped sometimes, or even dived in. As for me, I feel like I live in there at times. Maybe we all do. Maybe if there's any beauty in my life, it's the climbing out.

Like always, Steve was pretty quick to come down once we arrived at his apartment. He was on the balcony, raised his head, and next thing, he was with us, keys in hand. Steve's never been late for a single thing in his life.

He chucked his gear in the boot and we left.

We took Cleveland Street, which is always a bit choked, even on Sundays, and the radio was quiet as Steve drove. People cut him off and buses pulled out in front of him, but nothing moved him. He never blew the horn or yelled. To Steve, such things were irrelevant.

It was good for me to be at the ground at Maroubra that day. It was good to watch Steve and his ways. Just like the words I'd been writing made me feel and see things differently, it also gave me a greater curiosity. I wanted to see the way people moved and spoke and the reactions they were given. Steve was a good person to take notice of.

There was a rope fenced around the field and from where Sarah and I stood, I could see Steve approach the other members of his team. Every one of them looked his way and said something very briefly. Only one or two spoke with him longer. He stood at the edge of them and I could tell he wasn't close with them. With any of them. Yet, they liked him. They respected him. If he wanted it, he could have laughed with them and been the one that everyone listened to.

But it meant nothing there.

Not to Steve.

In the game, though, when he said he wanted the ball, he would get it. When something big was needed, Steve would do it. In the easy games the others would shine, but when things were hard, Steve was there, even if it was on his own.

They got ready and there was a lot of shouting and carrying on from the dressing sheds and both teams ran out. Steve was the captain of his team, and like I thought he would, he spoke a lot more on the field. Never yelling. I could just always see him mentioning something to another player or telling him what he had to do. Each one listened.

It was three o'clock when the game started.

The crowd was pretty big, with most of them drinking beer or eating meat pies or both. Many of them shouted things out, often losing food or spit from their mouths.

As was often the case, there was a brawl in the first few minutes, which Steve stayed right out of.

There was a guy who leaped up and hit him around the throat, and everyone ran in. Punches collided with skin, and fists were cut up on teeth.

Steve only got up and walked away.

He crouched down.

He spat.

Then he got up, took the penalty, and ran twice as hard.

They called his name incessantly.

'Wolfe. Watch Wolfe.'

They would send a few guys to take care of him every time, making sure to hurt him.

Each time Steve returned to his feet and kept going.

It made Sarah and me smile, as Steve sliced through them a few times and set up other people to score. By half time, his team was well in front. It was late in the second half when the importance of the day occurred.

The sky was a heavy grey and it was about to rain.

People were huddling now, in the cold.

A slippery wind was sliding across the air.

Kids kicked a ball and chased it behind us, with tomato sauce glued to the corners of their mouths, and scabs on their knees.

Steve was lining up a shot at goal from as far out on the field as you could get, right where the opposition supporters stood.

They mocked him.

Swore at him.

Told him he was useless.

As he moved in to kick the goal, a can of beer was thrown at his head. Beer flew out of it and the can slapped my brother on the side of his face.

He stopped.

Mid-step.

He froze.

In no rush, he bent down, picked up the can, and studied it. He turned to the group where it came from who were quiet almost immediately, and without looking at them again, he gently placed the can on the ground, out of the way, and lined the kick up again.

The crowd watched as Steve moved in and kicked the ball.

It rose up and soared through the posts, and Steve turned to face the people at his side. He stared at them for a few seconds, then returned to the game, leaving the beer can, half full, half empty and half hearted as it lay abandoned next to the sideline.

As I watched the end of the incident, I couldn't

help but notice that Steve's stare wasn't angry in any way. If anything, it was amused. He could have done anything he wanted. He could have said anything. He could have spat at them or hurled the can right back at them.

But that was something *they* could have done just as easily.

There was no way they could have walked in again, taken the shot, put it straight through the middle, and then stared as if to say, 'Well? Have you got anything else for me?'

That was how he beat them.

That was how he won.

He did the only thing they weren't capable of themselves.

When I realized that, I couldn't help but laugh, which made Sarah do the same, and we were the only people laughing in the whole ground. For everyone else, the game went on.

The game went on, the rain held off, and Steve's team won by a country mile.

When it was over, he said his goodbyes and that maybe he'd go for a drink with the other players, though everyone knew he wouldn't. We were going home.

There was more silence in the car than anything else, and I don't know about Steve or Sarah, but I couldn't stop thinking about the thrown beer can. I kept seeing the ball soar through the posts and the content stare on Steve's face. Even when Sarah reached for the dashboard and sang with the radio, it was the memory of that stare that spoke loudest through my mind. His face was the same now as he drove, and in some strange way, I think Steve was also thinking about it. I was even expecting him to smile, but he never did.

Instead, we were all pretty quiet, until Steve dropped us home.

'Thanks,' Sarah said.

'No worries. Thanks for coming.'

As I was about to get out of the car myself, Steve stopped me.

He stopped me with, 'Cam?'

'Yeah?'

He looked into the mirror and I could see his eyes as he talked to me.

'Just hang on a minute.'

This had never happened before, so I was unsure of what to expect. Would he tell me what the stare had meant, or how it felt to make those people look so stupid? Would he give me a guide on how to be a winner?

Of course not.

Or, at least, not like that.

His eyes were soft and honest as he spoke and it was strange for me to be feeling this way about Steven Wolfe.

He said, 'When I was your age, there were these four other blokes who beat me up. They took me round the back of a building and beat me up for some reason I'll never know.' He stopped a moment and he wasn't emotional in any way. He wasn't telling me some sob story about how other kids hated him and this was why he'd turned out the way he did. He was just telling me something. 'When I was lyin' there, all crumpled up, I vowed that each one of them was going to get his share of what they all did to me. I went over it in my mind and thought about what I wanted to do. Every morning, every night; and when I was ready, I went to them, one by one, and beat the absolute crap out of them. By the time I'd got to three of them, the last one tried to make peace.' The eyes sharpened a little, remembering. 'I bashed him too, even better than the other three.'

He stopped.

He stopped talking and I waited for more, until I realized that was it, and I nodded to my brother.

At the eyes in the mirror.

For a moment, I wondered, *Why is he telling me this?*

He didn't look proud or happy. Maybe just that same expression of contentment as before. Or maybe he was just glad he'd told somebody, because it sure didn't seem like he'd tell a whole load of people what he'd just told me. I couldn't be sure. As usual.

Finally, when I got out of the car, I wondered if anyone knew my brother. I wondered if Sal knew him.

I just knew that Steve was talking to me that day and it felt all right.

No, it felt good.

When he left, I waved to him but he was already halfway up the street. In the house, Octavia was sitting in our kitchen.

Rube wasn't.

They were as good as over.

She looked beautiful.

There must be thousands of alleys in this city.

Dark alleys everywhere.

In many of them, people have fought, cutting each other down and placing punches and kicks to bodies that have already fallen . . .

But what about the alleys in a person?

In a boy?

In a human?

How many times have I beaten myself down? I wonder. How many times have I lain there, in one of those alleys, between buildings that shiver and houses who slouch, their hands fixed in their pockets, doing nothing?

Tonight, I run through those alleys.

Past wounded cars.

Down grimly lit stairways.

Till I'm there.

I feel it.

Know it.

I see myself, lying there, at the bottom of the deepest, darkest alley. A slight breeze wades across the floor of it. It whispers to the rubbish, then picks it all up and moves it along.

Get up, I tell me.

Get up.

Slowly, I do, I make myself realize that it's OK to be Cameron Wolfe, and desire reaches through me again.

I realize that there's no one else in these alleyways, to beat me down or help me up.

There's only me.

6

Three words:

God damn Miffy.

I wasn't really in the mood for walking him, especially when I had to wait around quite a while for Rube.

At first, I sat in the kichen with Octavia.

She didn't look too impressed with things, considering she and Rube were supposed to be going out that afternoon. It must have slipped Rube's mind. At least, that was what he told her. Me, though? I knew Rube was away from her on purpose. I'd seen him do this before.

Come in late.

Argue.

Tell them he doesn't need this garbage.

It was a pretty good technique for Rube. He didn't mind being the villain.

There were leftovers on offer, but Octavia didn't stay for them. I walked out with her and we remained on the front porch a while, talking, and even managing to laugh now and then. Next door, I think Miffy could hear us and was expecting his walk. He sounded agitated at first, then started going off his nut.

'I'll just go get him,' I said, and quickly went next door to pick up the little bastard.

When we got back, I noticed Octavia was shivering.

As she stroked the dog, I took off my jacket and offered it to her. She accepted it, and soon after she said, 'It's warm, Cam.' She looked just past me. 'It's the warmest I've felt for a while . . .'

In a way, I hoped she wasn't just talking about the jacket, but it was better not to think that way. When you think like that, you end up standing outside people's houses, waiting for something that never comes.

She gave it back when we walked down to the gate and I opened it for her.

The moon was stuck to the sky and Octavia said, 'There's no point coming back really, is there?'

'Why?' I replied.

'Don't why me, Cameron.' She looked away and glanced back. 'Don't worry about it.' Even when she leaned onto the gate with her hands and her voice became unsteady, Octavia looked great, and I don't mean that in a dirty kind of way. I just mean that I liked her. I felt sorry for her, and for what Rube was doing to her. Her eyes smiled at me, for just a moment. One of those hurt smiles a person gives you to let you know they're OK, even though they're far from it.

After that she left.

When she was just past the gate, I asked, 'Octavia?'

She turned round.

'Y' gonna come back?'

'Maybe.' She smiled. 'One day.'

She walked along our street and it was cold and brutal and beautiful. For a few seconds, I hated my brother Rube for what he was doing to her.

Also, watching her walk slowly up our street, I remembered what Rube had said about Octavia and him following me one day when I walked over to Glebe and stood outside Stephanie's house. I could clearly see the image of them looking at me. Looking at me looking. She must have thought I was pathetic. A bit of a lonely bastard, as Rube put it. Maybe now, as she walked up the street, she knew how I felt.

Somehow, though, I understood that it was thoughts of Rube that filled her. Not thoughts of me. Maybe she was thinking of his hands on her, the thrill of it. Maybe it was laughter she remembered, or the words of a conversation. I would never know. I sat down again and Miffy jumped on my lap. As I watched Octavia, Miffy watched me, and when the girl had disappeared completely, the dog was giving me a certain look.

'What?' I asked him, but of course, he didn't answer. The dog looked like he'd genuinely caught me out, but soon enough, he returned to his usual disgusting self, yawning in my face. Your breath smells like a cesspool,' I said, and we waited for Rube.

He came in late for dinner and the old man gave him a good serve for it, as well as for leaving Octavia out to dry. I made sure to keep out of it. All I did was hang around with Miffy until Rube came out.

It was absolutely bloody freezing now and I wasn't in the mood.

The air was cold enough for us to wear our hoods indefinitely, and to watch the smoke pour from our mouths when we breathed.

Smoke came from Miffy's mouth too, especially

when he had a bit of a coughing fit. That was when we quickened the pace for home.

Later, we watched TV.

I looked over at my brother. He could sense it.

'What?' he said.

I was on the couch and Rube was in the worn-through chair.

'Is Octavia gone?'

He looked.

First away. Then back at me.

Yes.

That was the answer and Rube knew he didn't have to say it.

'There a new one?'

Again, he didn't have to answer.

'What's her name?'

He waited a while, then said it. 'Julia . . . but relax, Cam – I haven't done anything yet.'

I nodded.

I nodded and swallowed and I wished hard that it didn't have to be this way, for Octavia. I couldn't have cared less about Rube at this point. I thought only of the poor girl, and I thought of a time a few years ago when Sarah got dumped by this one particular guy. I remembered how shattered she was, especially when she found out there was another girl.

Rube and I hated the guy who did that.

We wanted to kill him.

Rube especially.

Now that guy was Rube.

For a moment, I nearly mentioned it, but all I did was sit there stupidly and look at Rube's face, side-on. There was no remorse in him. Almost no trace of thought about what he was doing.

Julia.

I could only wonder what she'd be like.

The only problem for Rube was that Octavia wanted to find things out for sure, so she came over again during the week.

They went out to the yard, and after a few minutes, she came back through the house on her own. When she saw me, she said, 'I'll see you, Cameron,' and again, she gave me that courageous smile – the one I saw the other night. Only this time, her green eyes were soaked more definitely, the water rising higher, only just managing not to fall out. She gathered herself and we stood in the hall and she said one last time, 'I'll see you around.'

'No you won't,' and I smiled back at her. We

both knew that people didn't see Cameron Wolfe – at least not unless they walked through the streets of the city a lot.

This time, when she left, she told me not to come out, but secretly, I stood on the front porch and watched her disappear.

'I'm sorry,' I whispered.

I figured that was the last time I'd ever see Rube's girl Octavia.

I was wrong.

WALK ON

At times I've wondered harder than usual about the girl in Glebe, where I constantly wait in the guttered city street. I wonder if she ever sees me.

I wonder if she sees me, knows me, or even likes the fact that I stand outside her house, or sit, waiting in vain. I wonder when I walk away if she might be pulling the curtain just slightly aside to watch me leaving.

God, I imagine it so hard.

So hard that it claws me.

Yet, I never turn round.

I just keep walking on because that's what I do. I never speak or shout or show anyone I'm there. I never allow my hand to form a fist and knock on the wood of her frightening front door.

Me?

I just walk on and never turn round.

And do you know why?

It's because I'm afraid she won't be there, watching for me.

When I walk on without looking, at least there's still some hope.

7

Julia was, of course, an absolute scrubber. There's not a whole lot more I can say about her. A scrubber (in case you don't know) is a girl who might be described as kind of slutty or festy, yet still without being a complete prostitute or anything like that. She chews gum a lot. She might drink excessively and smoke for show. She'll call you a faggot, poofter, or wanker with a lovely smirk on her face. She'll wear tight-arse jeans and good cleavage and she won't care too much if her headlights are on. Jewellery: moderate to heavy, maybe with a nose ring or eyebrow ring for rebellious originality. Then there's the makeup. At times it's *bucketed* on, especially if there's a bit of acne involved on her face, although more often than not, a scrubber isn't too bad-looking at all. She just has a tendency to make herself ugly, by what she says and what she does.

And Julia?

What can I say?

She was beautiful. She was blonde.

And she was a scrubber and a half.

'So this is Cameron,' she said when she first saw me. She was chewing that low-sugar gum that dentists highly recommend.

'Hey,' I said, and Rube winked at me. I knew what the wink meant. Something like, *Not bad, huh?* or, *You wouldn't knock her back, would y'?* or even simply, *Pretty good handfuls, ay?* The bastard.

As you can imagine, I got out of there pretty quick smart, because that girl annoyed the crap out of me very bloody fast. My only hope was that Rube wouldn't take her to see me staring at that Stephanie girl's house. Octavia, I could handle, beause she at least had a bit of class about her. A bit of niceness. But not this one. She'd most likely call me a bit of a lonely bastard as well. Or maybe she'd say something like, 'Get a life,' or repeat something Rube had previously said, hoping his charisma would rub off on her. No way. I wouldn't give her a chance. Not this one (even though *Christ*, I thought at one stage, *take a look at her*. She had an *Inside Sport* body if ever I'd seen one).

But no.

I'd made up my mind.

Rather than hang around them like a bad smell, I decided to go to the movies and hang around like a bad smell there instead.

On a cold, windy Saturday, when Dad didn't need me, I saw three movies on the one day, before going over to Glebe for a while, and then home. In the night, I went down to our basement and wrote for a while, feeling everything that was me shift and turn inside.

I was in bed for quite a while when Rube came in and slumped down on his own bed across from me. When I got up to turn off the light, he said, 'Well, Cam?'

'Well what?'

'What are your thoughts?'

'On what?'

'On Julia.'

'Well,' I began, but I didn't want to congratulate him on her, and I didn't want to interfere either. The injured darkness of the room swayed and stumbled and I said, 'She's OK, I guess.'

'OK?' He raised his voice excitedly. 'She's pretty bloody brilliant if you ask me.'

'But I didn't ask you, did I?' I stated. 'You asked *me* and I told you the answer.'

'Smart-arse.'

I laughed.

'Are you tryin' to start somethin'?'

'Of course not.'

'Well you better bloody not . . .'

Rube's voice trailed off and he fell asleep, letting the night throb around me, alone.

I lay there, not sleeping for hours – thinking about the cover model on the magazine at the barbers, then an exotic supermodel I saw on an ad at the movies. In my mind, I was with them. In them. Alone. For a while I even thought of Julia, but that was too much. I mean, there's perversion and there's perversion. Even for me.

In the morning, the previous night's conversation between Rube and me was forgotten. He ate slabs of bacon in the kitchen before going out again, while I stayed in because I had work due in at school next day.

Of course, I knew Rube was with Julia, and the pattern continued.

About two weeks went by, and everything was normal. Normal routine.

Dad was working hard, plumbing.

Mrs Wolfe was the same, cleaning people's

houses and doing a few cleaning shifts at the hospital.

Sarah did some overtime.

Steve kept winning at football, working in his office job and living in his apartment with Sal.

Rube went out with Julia.

And I still wrote my words, sometimes in our bedroom, sometimes in the basement. I also went over to Glebe quite a few times, more out of habit now than anything else.

Soon, though, a day came that changed everything.

It . . . I don't know how to explain it.

It all seemed so normal, but slightly off-centre at the same time.

I walked the city street, as usual.

I made my way over to the suburb of Glebe, without even thinking about where I was walking.

I went there, sat there, stood there, waited there, even begged there for something, anything to happen.

It was a Thursday, and in the dying moments of day, when the last rays of light stood up to be killed in the sky, I could feel someone behind me, just to the side. I could feel a presence, a shadow, standing just obscured behind a tree.

I turned round.

I looked.

'Rube?' I asked. 'That you, Rube?'

But it wasn't Rube.

I was sitting down against the small brick fence when I saw the person step into the last remnants of light, and walk slowly towards me. It was Octavia.

It was Octavia and she walked over and sat next to me.

'Hi, Cameron,' she said.

'Hi, Octavia.' I was shocked.

Silence bent down then, just for a moment, and whispered to each of us.

My heart threw itself to my throat.

Then, down.

Down.

She looked into the window I'd been staring at. Stephanie's window.

'Nothing?' she asked, and I knew what she meant.

'No, not tonight,' I answered.

'Any night?'

I couldn't help it.

I promise you, I couldn't . . .

A huge stupid tear rose up and fell out of my eye. It stammered down my face to my mouth and I could taste it. I could taste the saltiness of it, on my lips.

'Cameron?'

I looked at her.

'You OK?' she asked.

And all I did from there was tell her the truth.

I said, 'She's not comin' out tonight, or any other night, and there's nothing I can do about it.' I was even moved to quote Rube. 'Y' feel what y' feel, and that girl doesn't feel a thing for me. That's all there is to it . . .' I looked away, at the dying sky, attempting to pull myself together.

I began wondering exactly why I'd chosen this Glebe girl as the one I wanted to please, to drown in.

'Cam?' asked Octavia.

'Cam?'

She kept wanting me to look at her, but I still wasn't ready. Instead, I stood up and stared into the house. The lights went on. The curtains were drawn, and the girl, as always, was nowhere to be seen.

Yet, there was a girl next to me, who'd stood up now as well, and we were both beside the brick fence. She looked at me and made me look back. She asked one more time.

'Cam?'

Finally, I answered, quietly, timidly. 'Yeah?'

And Octavia's face cried out to me in the silent

city night as she asked, 'Would you come and stand outside my house instead?'

THE CHARCOAL SKY

Sometimes you go to the wrong place, but the right way comes and finds you. It might make you trip over it or speak to it. Or it might come to you when a day is stripped apart by night and ask you to take its hand and forget this wrong place, this illusion where you stand.

I think of the mess in my mind and the girl who walked through it to stand before me and let her voice come close.

I remember brick walls.

There are moments when you can only stand and stare, watching the world forget you as you remove yourself from it — when you overcome it and cease to exist as the person you were.

It calls your name, but you're gone.

You hear nothing. See nothing.

You've gone somewhere else. You've gone somewhere to find a different definition of yourself, and it's a place where nothing else can touch you. Nothing else can swing on your thoughts. It's only yourself, flat against the charcoal sky, for one moment.

Then flat on the earth again, where the world doesn't

recognize you any more. Your name is what it always was. You look and sound like you always did, yet you're not the same, and when a city wind begins to call out, its voice doesn't only hit the edges.

It connects.

It blows into you, rather than in spite of you.

Sometimes you feel like it's calling out for you.

8

She broke into me.

It was that simple.

Her wounds reached into me, grabbed my spirit by the heart, and reefed it from my body.

It was the words and the voice, and Octavia and me. And my spirit, on the silent, shadow-stricken street. I could only watch her, as slowly, she collected my hand and placed it gently in hers.

I took all of her in.

It was cold and her smoky breath flowed from her mouth. She smiled and her hair kept falling over her face, so beautiful and true. She suddenly had the most human eyes I'd ever seen, and the slight movements of her mouth whispered without the words. I could feel her pulse in my hand, beating gently onto my skin. Her shoulders were slight, and she stood with me on the city street that was slowly flooding with darkness. Her hand was holding onto me. She was waiting.

Silent Howls howled through me.

The street lights flickered on.

I remain still. Completely still, looking at her. Looking at the truth of her, standing before me.

I wanted to pull myself out and let my words spill onto the footpath, but I said nothing. This girl had just asked me the most brilliant question in the world and I was completely speechless.

'Yes,' I wanted to say. I wanted to shout it and pick her up and hold her and say, 'Yes. Yes. I'll come and stand outside your house any time,' but I didn't say anything. My voice found its way into my mouth but it never made it out. It always stumbled somewhere, then became lost, or was swallowed again.

The moment was cut open. It fell in pieces all around me, and I had no idea what would happen next, whether it would come from Octavia or me. I wanted to crouch down and pick up every piece of it and put it in my pockets. In a way, somewhere close to me, I could hear the voice of my spirit, telling me what to say, or what to do, but I couldn't understand it. The silence around me was too strong. It overwhelmed me, until I noticed her fingers wrapping tighter in mine for just a moment.

Then gone.

Slowly, she let her hand come loose, and it was over.

My hand fell back and gently slapped my side from the impact of her letting go.

She looked into me and then away.

Was she hurt? Did she expect me to speak? Did she want me to hold her hand again? Did she want me to pull her into me?

Questions lunged at me, but still I didn't get close enough to do anything. I simply stood there like a hapless, hopeless fool, waiting for something to change.

In the end it was Octavia's voice that stamped out the burning silence of the night.

A quiet, courageous voice.

She said, 'Just . . .' She hesitated. 'Just think about it, Cam,' and after a moment of thought and a last glance into me, she turned and walked away.

I watched.

Her legs.

Her feet, walking.

Her hair, echoing down her back in the dark.

I also remembered her voice, and the question, and the feeling I felt rising up through me. It shouted in me and warmed me and chilled me and threw itself down inside me. Why didn't I say anything?

Why didn't you say anything? I abused myself.

I could hear her footsteps now.

They lifted and scratched just slightly as she walked away in the direction of the train station.

'Cameron.'

A voice called to me.

'Cameron!'

I remember clearly that my hands were in my pockets, and when I looked over to my right, I swear I could make out the figure of my spirit, also standing against the brick fence, also with its hands in its pockets. It looked at me. It stared. It said more words.

'What the hell are you doing?' it asked me.

'What?'

'What do you mean *what*? Aren't you going after her?'

'I can't.' I looked down, at my old shoes and the jaded bottom sleeves of my jeans. I just looked and spoke. 'It's too late now anyway.'

My spirit came closer. 'Bloody hell, boy!' the words were brutal. They made me look up and stare, to find the face connected to the voice. 'You stand and wait outside some girl's place who couldn't care less, and when something real arrives, you fall apart! What kind of person *are* you?'

It shut up then.

The voice ended abruptly.

What it wanted to say was said, and we resumed standing against the fence, with our hands in our pockets, and silence feeding on our mouths.

A minute passed, and another. Time scratched itself through my thoughts, like the sound of Octavia's feet.

Finally, I moved.

It was after about fifteen minutes.

I took a final stare at the house, knowing it was probably the last time I would ever see it, and I began walking towards Redfern Station, under the electric wires, and through the cold of the street. The leaded windows of houses glimmered when the streetlights rushed at them, and I could hear my feet lifting and then clawing down onto the road as I started running. Behind me somewhere, I could hear the footsteps and breathing of my spirit. I wanted to beat it to the station. I had to.

I ran.

I let the cold air splash into my lungs as I thought the name *Octavia* over and over. I ran till my arms ached as hard as my legs and my head throbbed with the blood rushing into it.

'Octavia,' I said.

To myself.

I kept running.

Past the university.

Past the abandoned shops.

Past a few guys who looked like they might try to rob me.

'Come on,' I told myself when I thought I was slowing down, and I looked hard into the distance to see the legs and footsteps of Octavia.

When I made it to the station there were hordes of people pouring through the gates and I managed to slip through between a guy with a suitcase and a woman holding flowers. I went to the Illawarra line and sprinted down the escalator, past all the suits, the briefcases, and the different day-old perfumes and hair spray.

I made it to the bottom, nearly tripping.

Look at this bloody crowd! I thought, but slowly edged my way along the platform. When the train arrived all the people crammed and crushed and shook their heads when I got in their way. There was even a pretty bad smell like someone's underarm sweat. It licked me in the face, but still I looked and rushed through the crowd.

'Get out of the way,' someone snarled, and I was left with no other choice.

I got on the train.

I got on and stood in the packed middle compartment, right next to a guy with a moustache who was obviously the owner of the putrid underarm sweat. We both held onto the greasy metal pole until both the train and I got moving.

'Excuse me,' I said. 'Sorry,' and I made my way through the carriage downstairs. I figured I'd do all the lower levels of the train first and come back on the upper levels. This was the only train going to Hurstville. She had to be on it.

She wasn't in the carriage I got in on, or the next.

I opened the doors between each carriage and went through, with the cold tunnel air coughing around me before I entered the next carriage. Once I nearly slammed the door in my spirit's face as it closed in on me.

'There!'

I heard its voice point her out to me in the crowd of humans locked up in the suburban train.

I saw her just after the train rattled and burst out of the tunnel and into the paler darkness of the night. She was standing, just like I'd been standing a few carriages back, but facing the other way. From the lower level of the train, I could see her legs.

Footstep.

Footstep.

I edged my way closer and made it to the stairs and started climbing them.

Soon I could see all of her.

She stood and looked out the smeared window of the train. I wondered what thoughts she was thinking.

I was close, and I could see her neck and the movement of her breathing. I saw her fingers holding the pole as the train stuttered and the lights flooded and blinked.

Octavia, I said inside.

My spirit shoved me forward.

'Go on,' it said, but it didn't dare me, order me, or demand anything any more. It was just telling me what was right, and what I needed to do.

'All right,' I whispered.

I walked closer and stood behind her.

Her flannel shirt.

The skin of her neck.

The ruffled streams of hair landing on her back.

Her shoulder . . .

I reached out and touched her.

She turned round and I looked into her and a feeling lurched in me. God, she looked beautiful. I heard my voice. It said, 'I'll stand outside your house, Octavia.' I even smiled. 'I'll come and stand there tomorrow.'

That was when she closed her eyes for a moment and smiled back.

She smiled and said, 'That'd be good, Cam.' The voice was quiet.

I moved closer and grabbed hold of her shirt at her stomach and held onto her, relieved.

At the next stop, I told her I'd better get out.

'See you tomorrow?' she asked.

I nodded.

The train doors opened and I got out. When they closed I had no idea what station I was at, but as the train pulled and dragged itself along, I walked with it, still looking into her through the window.

When the train was gone I stood there, eventually realizing how cold it was on the platform.

Something struck me.

My spirit.

It was gone.

I searched everywhere for it, until I realized.

It didn't get off the train with me. It was still in the carriage, with Octavia.

TRACKS

A crowded train drags itself through me.

I own it now. I live inside the carriages, letting them carry me home.

If I stay inside long enough, the train slowly empties, until it's just her and me standing inside it, under the flickering fluorescent lights and above the metallic shifting of the wheels, rolling over the tracks.

The train breathes.

It speaks.

Its voice is made up of memory and the words of now.

Sparks flick and fall from above.

We stand.

I hold her by the shirt.

My spirit's at my shoulder, whispering.

Even when I get out of the train, I find myself running alongside it, bargaining with fatigue, and making sure I'll always remember it.

Finally, it goes too fast. It shivers in front of my eyes and fades, and I bend down, amongst the words. I allow my hands to fall to my knees. I suck the air hard. I can't breathe it quick enough, it tastes that good.

9

'Oi,' Rube said to me when I made it in that night. 'What the hell happened to you? You're a bit late, aren't y'?'

'I know.' I nodded.

'There's soup in the pot,' Mrs Wolfe cut in.

I lifted the lid off it, which is usually the worst thing you can ever do. It clears the kitchen, though, which was pretty useful that night, considering. I wasn't really in the mood to be answering questions, especially from Rube. What was I going to tell him? 'Ah, you know, mate. I was just out with your old girlfriend. You don't mind, do y'?' No way.

The soup took a few minutes and I sat and ate it alone.

As I ate, I started coming to terms with what had happened. I mean, it's not every day something like that happens to you, and when it does, you can't help but struggle to believe it.

Her voice kept arriving in me.

'Cameron?'

'Cameron?'

After hearing it a few times, I turned round to find Sarah talking to me as well.

'You OK?' she asked.

I smiled at her. 'Of course,' and we washed up.

Later, Rube and I went over and collected Miffy, walking him till he started wheezing again.

'He sounds bloody terrible. Maybe he's got flu or somethin',' Rube suggested. 'Or the clap.'

'What's the clap?'

'I'm not sure. I think it's some kind of sex disease.'

'Well I don't think he's got that.'

When we took him back over to Keith he said Miffy got fur balls a lot, which made sense, since that dog seemed to be made up of ninety per cent fur; a couple per cent flesh; a few per cent bones; and one or two per cent barking, whingeing and carrying on. Mostly fur, though. Worse than a cat.

We gave him a last pat and left.

On our front porch I asked Rube how the Julia girl was going.

'Scrubber,' I imagined him announcing, but knew he wouldn't.

'Ah, not bad, y' know,' he replied. 'She's not the best but she's not the worse either. No complaints really.' It didn't take long for a girl to go from brilliant to run-of-the-mill with Rube.

'Fair enough.'

For a moment, I almost asked how Octavia rated, but I wasn't interested in her the way Rube was, so there was no point. It wasn't important. For me, it was the way that thoughts of her could keep finding me that was important. I just couldn't stop thinking about her, as I convinced myself about everything that had happened.

Her appearance on the street in Glebe.

Her question.

The train.

All of it.

We sat there a while on the worn-out couch Dad put out there a few summers ago and watched the traffic amble by.

'What are youse starin' at?' a scrubberish sort of girl snapped at us as she idled past on the footpath.

'Nothin',' Rube answered, and we could only laugh a while as she swore at us for no apparent reason and continued walking.

My thoughts turned inward.

In each passing moment, Octavia found a way into me. Even when Rube started talking again, I was back on the train, pushing my way through the humans, the sweat and the suits.

'Are we workin' with Dad this Saturday?' Rube stamped out my thoughts.

'I'm pretty sure we are,' I said, and Rube got up and went inside. I stayed on the porch a fair while longer. I thought about the next night, and standing outside Octavia's house.

I didn't sleep that night.

The sheets stuck to me and I turned and got tangled in them. At one point, I even got up and just sat in the kitchen. It was past two in the morning then, and when Mrs Wolfe got up to go to the toilet, she came to see who was there.

'Hey,' I whispered.

'What are you doing?' she asked.

'I couldn't sleep.'

'Well, go back to bed soon, all right?'

I sat there a while longer, with the talkback radio show talking and arguing with itself at the kitchen table. Octavia filled me that whole night. It made me wonder if she was sitting in her own kitchen, thinking of me.

Maybe.

Maybe not.

Either way, I was going there the next day, and the hours were disappearing slower than I thought possible.

I returned to bed and waited. When the sun came up, I got up with it, and gradually, the day passed me by. School was the usual concoction of jokes, complete bastards, shoves, and a laugh here and there.

For a few anxious seconds in the afternoon, I wasn't sure what Octavia's last name was and feared I might not be able to look her up in the phone book. I was relieved when I remembered. It was Ash. Octavia Ash. When I got the address, I looked the street up on the map and found it to be about a ten-minute walk from the station, as long as I didn't get lost.

Maybe for comfort, I jumped the fence and gave Miffy a pat for a while. In a way, I was nervous. Nervous as hell. I thought of everything that might go wrong. Train derailment. Not being able to find the right house. Standing outside the *wrong* house. I covered all of it in my mind as I patted the ball of fluff that had rolled over and somehow smiled as I rubbed his stomach.

'Wish me luck, Miffy,' I said softly as I got up to

leave, but all he did was prop himself up and give me a look of *Don't you stop patting me, you lazy bastard*. I jumped the fence anyway, though, and went through the house. I left a note saying I might go to Steve's that night so no one would worry too much. (The odds were that I might end up there in any case.)

I was wearing the sort of thing I always wear. Old jeans, a jersey, my black spray jacket and my old shoes.

Before I left, I went to the bathroom and tried to keep my hair from sticking up, but that's like trying to defy gravity. My hair sticks up no matter what. Thick like dog's fur, and always slightly messy. There's just never a lot I can do about it. *Besides*, I thought, *I should just try to be like I was yesterday. If I was good enough yesterday I should be good enough today.*

It was settled. I was going.

I let the front door slam shut behind me and the flyscreen rattle. It was as if each door was kicking me out of the old life I'd lived in that house. I was being thrown out into the world, new. The broken, leaning gate creaked open, let me out, and I gently placed it shut. I was gone, and from down the street, maybe fifty metres away, I looked back for a second at the house where I lived. It wasn't the same any more. It never would be. I kept walking.

The traffic on the street waded past me, and at one point, when it all got blocked, a passenger from a cab spat out the window and it landed near my feet.

'Christ,' the guy said. 'Sorry, mate.'

All I did was look at him and say, 'No worries.' I couldn't afford to be distracted. Not today. I'd picked up the scent of a different life, and nothing was going to get me off it. I would hunt it down. I would find it, taste it, devour it. The guy could have spat in my face and I would have wiped it off and kept walking.

There would be no distractions.

No regrets.

It was still afternoon when I made it down to Central Station, bought my ticket, and headed for the underground. Platform twenty-five.

Standing there, I waited at the back of the platform till I felt the cold wind of the train pushing through the tunnel. It surrounded my ears until the roar entered me and slowed to a dull, limping sigh.

It was an old train.

A scabby one.

In the last carriage, downstairs, there was an old man with a radio, listening to jazz music. He said hello to me (a very rare event on any form of public transport), and I knew that things would have to go right today. I felt like I'd earned it.

My thoughts veered with the train.

My heart held itself back.

When Hurstville came, I stood up and made my way out, and to my amazement, I found Octavia's street without any problems. Usually when it comes to directions I'm an absolute shocker.

I looked at each house, trying to guess which one was number thirteen Howell Street.

When I made it, I found the house to be nearly as small as where I lived, and red brick. It was getting dark, and I stood there, waiting and hoping, hands in pockets. There was a fence and a gate, and a close-cut lawn with a path. I began wondering if she'd come out.

People came from the station.

They walked past me.

Finally, when the same darkness as the previous day overcame the street, I turned away from the house and faced the road, half sitting, half leaning on the fence. A few minutes later, she came.

I could barely hear the front door open or her footsteps coming towards me, but there was no mistaking the feeling of her behind me when she stopped and stood within reaching distance. I shiver even now as I remember the feeling of her cool hands on my neck, and the touch of her voice on my skin.

'Hi, Cameron,' she said, and I turned round to face her. 'Thanks for coming.'

'It's OK,' I spoke. My voice was dry and cracked open.

I smiled then, I remember, and my heart swam in its own blood. There was no holding back any more. In my mind, I had gone over moments like this a thousand times, and now that I was truly in one, there was no way I could blow it. I wouldn't allow myself.

I went along the fence and into the gate, and when I made it over to Octavia, I picked up her hand and held it in mine. I raised it to my mouth and kissed it. I kissed her fingers and her wrist as gently as my clumsy lips could.

Her eyes widened.

The expression on her face came that little bit closer.

Her mouth merged into a smile.

'Come on,' she said, leading me out the gate. 'We don't have long tonight,' and we moved onto the path.

We walked down the street to an old park, where I searched myself for things to say.

Nothing came.

All I could think of was utter crap like the weather and all that sort of thing, but I wasn't going to reduce myself to that. She still smiled at me, though, telling me silently that it was OK not to talk. It was OK not to win her over with stories or compliments or anything else I could say just to say *something*. She only walked and smiled, happier in silence.

In the park, we sat for a long time.

I offered her my jacket and helped her put it on, but after that, there was nothing.

No words.

No anything.

I don't know what else I expected, because I had absolutely no idea how to confront this. I had no idea how to act around a girl, because to me, what she wanted was completely shrouded in mystery. I didn't really have a clue. All I knew was that I wanted her. That was the simple part. But actually knowing what to do? How in the hell could I ever come close to coping with that? Can you tell me?

My problem came, I think, from being inside aloneness for so long. I always watched girls from afar, hardly getting close enough to smell them. Of course I *wanted* them, but even though I was miserable about not actually having them, it was also kind of a relief. There was no pressure. No discomfort. In a way, it was easier just to imagine what it would be like, rather than confront the reality of it. I could create ideal situations, and ways that I would act to win them over.

You can do anything when it's not real.

When it *is* real, nothing breaks your fall. Nothing gets between you and the ground, and that night, in the park, I had never felt so real. I'd never felt so lacking in control. It seemed to be the way it was, and the way it always would be.

Before, life was about getting girls (or hoping to).

Not about getting to know them, or actually *getting* what they were about.

Now, it was much different.

Now, it was about *one* girl, and working out what to do.

I thought for a while, trying to find the elusive breakthrough of what to say. Thoughts pinned me down, leaving me there, to think about it. In the end, I tried convincing myself that everything would turn out. Nothing turns on its own, though.

All right, I told myself, trying to pull myself

together. I even started listing the things I'd actually done right.

I'd chased her down on the train the day before.

I'd spoken to her and said I'd stand outside her house.

God, I'd even kissed her hand.

But now I had to talk, and I had nothing to say.

Why don't you have anything to say, you stupid bastard? I asked myself.

I begged inside me.

Several times.

The disappointment in myself was bitter as I sat on a splinter-infested park bench with her, wondering what to do next.

At one point I opened my mouth, but nothing came out.

In the end, I could only look at her and say, 'I'm sorry, Octavia. I'm sorry I'm so bloody useless.'

She shook her head, and I saw that she was disagreeing with me.

She said quietly, 'You don't have to talk at all, Cameron.' She looked into me. 'You'd never have to say a thing and I'd still know you're big-hearted.'

That was when the night burst open and the sky fell down, in slabs, around me.

I think about it hard — about silence and getting the girl.

Getting.

Getting.

When you're young and dirty, everything's about getting your hands on a girl . . . or at least, that's what people say. It may not be what they think, but it's what they tell you.

For me, though, it feels like more than that. I want to hear her, and know her.

I want to understand.

What to do.

What to say.

I don't want to stand in naked silence, pathetically unaware of how to be. I want to cut myself free. I want to shake myself away from the silence, and I want it now.

Yet, I think, as usual, I'll have to wait.

And you never know.

Maybe one day I'll understand.

One day I'll get the girl.

One day I might even get the world . . . but I doubt it.

10

Sarah knew.

She could tell by looking when I came in that night, she reckoned. She told me right away, when I tried to slip past her on my way down the hall to Rube's and my room.

It was funny.

Unbelievable.

How could she be so sure – so sure that when I came in, she could stop me and shove her hand to my heart and say with a grin and a whisper, 'Tell me, Cameron. What's the name of the girl who can make your heart beat this fast?'

I grinned back, shocked and shy, amazed.

'No one,' I denied.

'Huh,' and a short laugh.

Huh.

That was all she said, as she took her hand off me and turned away, still smiling.

'Good for you, Cameron.' That was what she said

as she walked away. She faced me, one last time. 'You deserve it. You really do, I mean it.'

She left me to stand there, remembering what happened right after the slabs of sky fell down around me.

For a while, Octavia and I remained on the bench, as the air grew colder. Only when she started shivering did we stand up and walk back to her house. At one point, her fingers touched mine, and she held on just faintly.

Before she went in, she said, 'I'll be down the harbour on Sunday, if you feel like coming. I'll be there around noon.'

'OK,' I replied, already imagining myself standing there, watching her play the harmonica with people throwing money onto her jacket. Bright blue sky. Climbing clouds. The hands of the sun, reaching down. I could see all of it.

'And Cameron?' she asked.

I returned from my vision.

'I'll wait for you.' She let her eyes hit the ground and arrive again, in mine. 'You know what I mean?'

I nodded, slowly.

She would wait for me, to talk, and to be with her

the way I could be. I guess we could only hope it would just be a matter of time.

'Thanks,' I said, and rather than let me watch her go inside, Octavia stayed at the gate and waved each time I turned round for one last glimpse of her. With every turn, I whispered, 'Bye, Octavia,' until I was round the corner, on my own again.

Memories of the ride home are shaded by the haziness of a train ride at night. The clacking of the train rolling and turning over the tracks still rides through me. It gives me a vision of myself sitting there, travelling back to where I came from, but a place that would no longer be the same.

It was strange how Sarah could sense it immediately.

She could see the change in me straight away, in the way I existed in our house. Maybe I moved or spoke differently, I didn't know. I *was* different, though.

I had my words.

I had Octavia.

In a way, it seemed like I wasn't pleading with myself any more. I wasn't begging for those scraps of all-rightness. I just told myself to be patient, because, finally, I was standing somewhere close to where I wanted to be. I'd fought for this, and now I was nearly there.

Much later in the night, Rube came home and collapsed like always into bed.

Shoes still on.

Shirt half undone.

There was a slight smell of beer, smoke, and his usual cheap cologne that he didn't need because the girls fell over him anyway.

Loud breathing. Smiling sleep.

It was typical Rube. Typical Friday night.

He also left the light on, as always, so I had to get up and switch it off.

We both knew good and well that Dad would be waking us in the morning when it was still dark. I also knew that Rube would get up, and he'd look rough and tired and yet still pretty damn good. He had a way of doing that, my brother, which annoyed the absolute hell out of me.

As I lay there, across from him, I wondered what he would say when he found out about Octavia and me. I went through a whole list of possibilities, because Rube was likely to say anything, depending on what was happening at the time, what had previously happened, and what was going to happen next. Some of the things I thought of were:

He'd slap me hard across the back of the head and say, 'What the hell are y' thinking, Cam?' Another slap. 'Y' don't do that sort of thing with y' brother's old girlfriend!' Another slap, and one more, just in case.

Then again, he might just shrug. Nothing. No words, no anger, no mood, no smile, no laugh.

Or he might pat me on the back and say, 'Well, Cam, it's about time you pulled y' finger out.'

Or maybe he'd be speechless.

No.

No chance.

Rube was never speechless.

If there was nothing he could think of saying, he'd most likely look at me and exclaim, 'Octavia!? Really!?'

I'd nod.

'Really!?'

'Yeah.'

'Well that's just bloody brilliant, that is!'

The situations merged through me as I fell down slowly into sleep. My dreams collected everything up until a hard hand shoved me awake at quarter past six the next morning.

The old man.

Clifford Wolfe.

'Time to get up,' said his voice, through the darkness. 'Wake that lazy bastard too.' He jerked his thumb over at Rube, but I could tell he was smiling. With Dad, Rube and me, calling each other bastards was a term of endearment.

The job was right on the coast, at Bronte.

Rube and I pretty much dug under the house all day, listening to the radio.

For lunch, we all walked down to the beach and Dad got the obligatory fish 'n' chips. When we were done, Rube and I went down to the shoreline to get the grease off our hands.

'Friggin' freezin',' Rube warned me about the water, but still he pooled it in his hands and threw it on his face and through his thick, sandy hair.

Along the shore, there were shells washed up.

I started shuffling through them and picking up the best ones to keep.

Rube looked over.

'What are y' doin'?' he asked.

'Just collectin' a few shells.'

He looked at me in disbelief. 'Are you a bloody poofter or somethin'?'

I glanced at the shells in my hands. 'What's wrong with it?'

'Christ!' he laughed. 'You are, aren't y'?'

I only looked over and laughed back, then picked up a shell that was clean and smooth and had a gentle tiger pattern on it. In the centre there was a small hole, for looking through.

'Look at this one,' I said, holding it out to him.

'Not bad,' Rube admitted, and as we stared over the ocean, my brother said, 'You're OK, Cameron.'

All I could do was stare a few seconds longer before we turned back. The old man had already given us an 'oi' to get us back to work. We walked over the sand and back up the street. Later that day, Rube told me some things. About Octavia.

It started innocently enough, with me asking how many girlfriends he reckoned he'd had.

'I wouldn't know,' he answered me. 'I never counted 'em. Maybe twelve, thirteen.'

For a while, there was only the sound of the digging, but I could tell my brother, like me, was going over the girls in his head, touching each girl with the fingers of his mind.

In the middle of it, I had to ask him.

I said, 'Rube?'

'Shut up – I'm tryin' to concentrate.'

I ignored him and kept going. I'd started now and I wasn't going to stop. I asked, 'Why'd you get rid of Octavia?'

Rube stopped digging, and I could tell he was debating what to say in his mind. He gave me the answer. 'To tell you the truth, Cam. *She* quit *me*. That night when she came back I was expecting her to cry and carry on like some of the others.' He shook his head now. 'But I was wrong. She just came and really gave it to me. She said I wasn't worth the effort.' He shrugged a moment, then spoke again. 'The funny thing was, when she left, she looked so brilliant, I almost felt like running after her.' For the first time then, he met me in the eyes. 'That's never happened before. It was like, I don't know, Cam. I think it was the first time I felt like I'd lost something good.'

I nodded and stayed silent, and even started digging a bit prematurely. I thought about loss and gain and everything in between. And naturally, I forced myself to forget about it.

What confused me most was how Rube could still be so calm about it. If it were me in his shoes, the agony of someone like Octavia breaking up with me would have left me in strips and pieces on the ground. It would have broken me.

But that was me.

For Rube, the next best thing came along, so he took it, and I guess there was nothing wrong with that. The only problem for Rube now, it seemed, was that the Julia girl came with some excess baggage. She'd come at a price.

'Apparently she was still with some other bloke when she started up with me,' he stated matter-of-factly. 'Some honcho from out Canterbury way.'

'Honcho?' I asked. 'What the hell's a honcho?'

Rube leaned on his shovel. 'You know all those guys out there – gangs, nicknames, chains. All that crap.' He smiled a moment, maybe looking forward to the challenge. 'And apparently this guy's after killin' *me* for his girl losing interest in him. It's not like I did anything wrong, for Jesus' sake. It's not like the girl told me she was already taken.'

'Just be careful,' I told him. Once again, he could tell by the tone of my voice that I wasn't a big fan of this Julia girl. He asked me straight out.

He said, 'You don't like her, do y'?'

I shook my head.

'Why not?'

You hurt Octavia to get her, I thought, but said, 'I don't know. I've just got a bad feeling about this one, that's all.'

'Don't worry about me,' Rube responded. He looked over and gave me his usual grin – the one that always says everything will be all right. 'I'll survive.'

As it turned out, I kept just the one shell from the beach. It was the one with the tiger pattern. At home, I held it against the light from our bedroom window. I already knew what I'd do with it.

It was in my pocket the next day when I walked down to Central and caught the train over to Circular Quay. The harbour water was a rich blue, with the ferries trudging over it, cutting it, then allowing it to settle. On the docks, there were people everywhere, and plenty of buskers. The good, the brilliant and the hopeless. It took a while, but I finally saw her. I saw Octavia on the walkway to the Rocks, and I could see the people milling around her, drawn to the powerful voice of her mouth organ.

I arrived when she was just finishing a song and people were putting money into her old jacket, which was spread out on the ground. She smiled at them and said thanks, and most of the people moved slowly on.

Without noticing I was there, she went straight into another song, and again, a crowd began to gather around her. This time it wasn't quite as big. The sun surrounded her wavy hair, and I watched intently as her lips slid across the instrument. I looked at her neck, her soft flannel shirt, and stole visions of her hips and her legs through gaps in the crowd. In the song, I could hear her words, 'It's OK, Cameron, I can wait.' I also heard her calling me big-hearted, and hesitantly at first, then without thinking, I moved to the crowd and made my way through it.

Breathing, stopping, and then crouching, I was the closest person in the world to Octavia Ash. She played her harmonica, and before her, I was kneeling down.

She saw me and I could see the smile overcome her lips.

My pulse quickened.

It burned in my throat as slowly, I reached into my pocket, pulled out the tiger shell, and placed it gently onto the jacket where all the money was strewn.

I placed it there and the sun hit it, and just as I was about to turn round to make my way back through the crowd, the music stopped. In the middle of the song it was cut short.

The world was silent and I turned again to look up at a girl who stood completely still above me.

She crouched down, placed her harmonica amongst the money, and picked up the shell.

She held it in her hand.

She pulled it to her lips.

She kissed it, softly.

Then, with her right hand, she pulled me towards her by my jacket and kissed me. Her breath went into me, and the softness, warmness, wetness and openness of her mouth covered me, as a sound from outside us burst through my ears. For a moment, I wondered what it was, but fell completely into Octavia again as she poured through me. We both kneeled, and my hands held onto her hips. Her mouth kept reaching for mine, touching me. Connecting. Her right hand was on my face now, holding me, keeping me close.

The roaring sound continued around us, forming walls to make this a world within the rest of the world. Suddenly I knew what it was. The sound was clear and clean, and magnificent.

It was the sound of humans clapping.

CLAPPING HANDS

What is it about the sound of clapping hands?

It's only skin against slapping skin, so why can it make a tide turn in you? Why can it break on top of you and lift you up at the same time?

Maybe it's because it's one of the most noble things humans do with their hands.

I mean, think about it.

Humans make fists with their hands.

They use them to fight, to steal things, to hurt each other.

When people clap, it's one of the few times they stand together and applaud other people.

I think they're there to keep things. They hold moments together, to remember.

11

It's the best thing anyone's ever given me,' she said, holding it up and looking at me through the hole. She kissed me again, lightly on the mouth and once on my neck. She whispered in my ear. 'Thanks, Cameron.' I loved her lips, especially when the sun hit them and she smiled at me. I'd never seen her smile like that when she was with Rube, and I hoped it was a smile she'd never been able to give to anyone else alive. I couldn't help it.

The people were gone now and we collected up the money from Octavia's jacket. It was just over fifty-six dollars. In my left jacket pocket, I still held all my words, including what I'd just written when she'd returned to playing. My fingers held them tightly, guarding them.

'Let's go,' she said, and we started walking along the water towards the bridge. Shadows of cloud lurked in the water, like holes the sun forgot about. The girl next to me still looked at the shell, and my heartbeat felt like fingers climbing over my ribs. Even when it slowed, there was still a force to it. I liked it.

Under the bridge, we sat down against the wall, Octavia with her legs outstretched, me with my knees held up to my throat. I glanced over at her and noticed the way the light touched her skin and handled the hair that fell into her face. It was the colour of honey. She had salty green eyes — the colour of the harbour on an overcast day — and she had tanned skin and a straight-teeth smile that got crowded on the right side when she opened her mouth further. (I'd never noticed that previously.) She had a smooth neck and the shins of her legs wore a few bruises. Nice knees and hips. I liked girls' hips, but I liked Octavia's especially. I . . .

It was there again.

Between us.

The silence.

There was only the sound of water throwing itself against the walls of the harbour, until finally, I looked over at Octavia and said quietly, 'I just wanted to . . .'

Pause.

A long pause.

She wanted to speak, I could sense it. I noticed it in the pleading of her eyes, and the slight movement of her lips. She was dying to say something but held back. I finished the sentence.

'I just wanted to say . . .' I cleared my throat, but it remained cracked. 'Thanks.'

'For what?'

I hesitated slightly. '. . . For wanting me.'

She looked over and placed her eyes in mine for just the briefest of seconds. Her fingers touched my wrist and made their way down to hold my own fingers in hers. She then said something very deliberately.

She smiled a moment and calmly said, 'I like your hair, Cameron. I like how it sticks up no matter how hard you try to keep it down. It's the one thing you can't hide.' She swallowed. 'But the rest of you is hidden. It's hidden behind your measured walk, the crushed collar of your jacket, and your awkward, nervous smile. You can kill me with that smile if you want.'

I looked over.

'Do you know that?' she asked again, almost accusingly.

'No.'

'Well it's true, but . . .'

'What?'

'Can't you see?' She squeezed my hand. 'I want more than that.' A tough kind of smile fought its way to her face. 'I just want to know you a bit, Cameron, that's all.'

Again, I noticed the sound of the water.

Rising.

Bashing against the wall before diving back down.

Finally, I nodded. I decided.

There was only one way to do this and now I had it.

I stood up and walked to the water.

I turned round.

The bridge towered over me and I started talking as I crouched down maybe ten metres away and looked into her.

Words flew from my mouth.

'My name's Cameron. I've always said that I wanted to drown inside a girl, inside her spirit, but I've never even come close – I've barely even touched a girl. I don't have friends. I live in the shadow of both my brothers – one for his single-minded focus on success, the other for his brilliance, rough smile, and ability to make people like him. I hope my sister won't just be another slab of flesh that some guy just picks up and throws a few dollars at to buy cheap lipstick but don't forget the beer. I work with my father on weekends and my hands get dirty and blistered. I get thoughts in my head of movies with sex scenes and about girls from school, model girls, a female teacher or two, girls in ads, girls on calendars, girls on TV shows who turn letters, girls in uniforms or corporate suits who sit on the train reading thick books with perfume smothered on their throats and perfect makeup. I walk around the city a lot and when I do, it feels like the soul of home. I love my brother Rube but I hate what he does to girls, especially when they're real girls like you who should have known better than to go out with him in the first place. I idolize Mrs Wolfe because she keeps us together and works like hell. She works harder than she should ever have to, and one day I want to do something brilliant for her like put her in first class on a plane to wherever she wants . . .' I remembered to breathe but forgot what I was going to say next.

I stopped talking and stood up, because my legs were getting sore from the crouching down. Slowly, I walked towards Octavia Ash, whose bruised shins were now held up by her folded arms.

'I—'

Again, I stopped, as I walked to her and crouched down in front of her. I could feel the blood collect again in my legs.

'What?' she asked. 'What is it?'

For a few seconds I wondered if I should do it or not, but before I allowed myself not to, I reached into the pocket of my jacket and pulled out clumps of paper and held them out to her, as if I were offering her everything I owned. On the paper were the words.

'These are mine,' I said, placing them in her outstretched hand. 'Open them and read them. They'll tell you who I am.'

She did as I asked, opening the small piece of writing that was my first. The only thing is, she read only the start of them. She handed the paper back to me and asked, 'Would you read them to me, Cameron?'

My thoughts kneeled down.

The breeze wandered between us and I sat next to her again and began reading the words I wrote back in Chapter One of this story.

'The city streets are lined with truth, and I walk through

them. *Sometimes,* they *walk through me . . .'* I read the page slow and true, exactly how it felt to me, as if it were oozing from me, and I said the last part just a touch louder. *'Yes, when that's done, I also want the everything that's her to fill up so much in front of me that it spills and shivers and gives, just like I'm prepared to do myself. But for now, happiness throws stones. It guards itself. I wait.'*

When I was finished, a final silence gripped us both and the sound of the paper folding up again sounded like something crashing. A look of feeling clutched at her face, holding it.

She waited a while, before gently speaking. 'You've never touched a girl before?'

'No.'

'Not till me?'

'No.'

'Could you do me a favour?' she asked.

I nodded, looking at her.

'Could you hold my hand?'

Feeling every part of it, I took Octavia's hand, and she came closer and rested her head on my shoulder. She put her leg over mine and hooked her foot under my ankle, linking us.

'I never thought I'd show anyone my words,' I said quietly.

'They're beautiful,' she spoke softly in my ear.

'They make me OK . . .'

Soon after, she moved in front of me, crossed her legs, and faced me, making me read everything I'd written so far. When it was over, she moved my hands across her stomach to hold her on the hips.

She said, 'You can drown inside me anytime, Cameron,' and she put her lips on mine again and let herself flow through the inside of my mouth. The pages were still in my hands, pressed against her as I held her hips, and I could feel her on top of me, breathing me in.

After a while, we got up and Octavia turned to me. She asked a serious question.

She leaned towards me and said, 'You feel like getting high?'

'High?' I asked.

'Yeah.' She smiled in a dangerous, self-mocking way, and I only began to understand why when we headed back towards the middle of the city, to the tower.

We entered the lift and it took us right to the top, with some English golf-pro-looking types, and a family on a Sunday outing. One of the kids kept stepping on my foot.

'Little bastard,' I felt like saying. If I had been with Rube I probably would have, but with Octavia, I only looked at her and implied it. She nodded back as if to say, 'Exactly.'

Once up there, we walked around the whole floor and I couldn't help but look for my own house, imagining what was happening there, and hoping, even praying, that everything was going OK. That extended to include everyone down there, as far as I could see, and as I always do when I pray to a God I wouldn't have a clue about, I stood there, lightly beating at my heart, without even thinking.

Especially this girl, though, I prayed. *Let her be OK, God. All right? All right, God?*

That was when Octavia noticed my fist lightly touching my heart. There was no answer from God. There was a question from the girl.

She asked, 'What are you doing?' I could feel the curiosity of her eyes on my face. 'Cameron?'

I stayed focused on the city sprawled out beneath us. 'Just sort of prayin', y' know?'

'For what?'

'Just that things will be OK.' I stopped, continued. Almost laughed. 'And I haven't been in a church for nearly seven years . . .'

We stayed up there for over an hour, walking around to see the whole city from this high up.

'I come up here a fair bit,' she told me. 'I like the height.' She even climbed to the carpeted step at the window and stood there, leaning forward onto the glass. 'You comin' up?' she asked, and I'll be honest – I tried, but no matter how much I wanted to lean forward onto that glass, I couldn't. I kept feeling like I was going to fall through.

So I sat there.

Only for a few seconds.

When she came back down she could see I wasn't doing too well.

'I wanted to,' I said.

'Don't worry, Cam.'

The thing was, I knew there was something I had to ask, and I did it. I even promised myself that this would be the last time I asked a question like this.

I said, 'Octavia?' I kept hearing her telling me that she came up here all the time. I heard it when I spoke the words, 'Did you bring Rube up here too?'

Slowly, she nodded.

'But he leaned on the glass,' I answered my own question. 'Didn't he?'

Again, she nodded. 'Yeah.'

I don't know why, but it seemed important. It was important. I felt like a failure because my older brother leaned on the glass and I couldn't. It made me feel hopeless in some way. Like I wasn't even half the guy he was.

All because he leaned on glass and I couldn't.

All because he had the neck and I didn't.

All because . . .

'That doesn't mean anything.' She shot down my thoughts. 'Not to me.' She thought for a moment and faced me. 'He leaned on the window, but he never made me feel like you do. He never stood outside my house. He never gave me any truth, the way you have with your pages there. He never gave me something he couldn't give to anyone else.' She struggled not to explain it, but to actually say it. 'The few times I've been with you, I feel like I'm kind of outside myself, you know?' She finished me. 'I don't want Rube. I don't want anyone else.' Her eyes ate me, quietly. 'I want you.'

I looked.

Down.

At my shoes, then back up, at Octavia Ash.

I went to say, 'Thanks,' but she stopped me by pushing her fingers up to my mouth.

'Always remember that,' she spoke. 'All right?'

I nodded.

'Say it.'

'All right,' I said, and her cool hands touched me on my neck, my shoulder, my face.

SOMETIMES YOU GET THE GIRL — SOMETIMES THE GIRL GETS YOU

Inside me, I'm high up, leaning forward onto glass.

It cracks.

It comes apart and falls open.

Momentum pushes me out and I'm being dragged to earth at a speed beyond my imagination.

I see the width of the world.

The farther I fall, the faster it turns, and around me, I see visions of everyone and everything I know. There's Rube and Steve, Sarah, Dad and Mrs Wolfe, Keith and Miffy, and Julia the Scrubber, looking seductive. Even the barber's there, chopping hair that litters down around me.

I think only one thing.

Where's Octavia?

As I get closer to the bottom, I notice that it's water I'm falling into. It's salty-green and smooth, until . . .

I'm driven through the surface and go deeper. I'm surrounded.

I'm drowning. I think. I'm drowning.

But I'm smiling too.

12

When I got home that Sunday night, Rube and I did the usual deed of walking Miffy. The hound was in even worse shape than usual. The coughing sounded deeper, like it was coming from his lungs.

When we got back I asked Keith if he was going to take him to the vet.

'I don't think this is fur balls,' I said.

Keith's reply was pretty short and simple. 'Yeah, I think I'd better. He looks shockin'.'

'Worse.'

'Ah, he's been like this before,' he explained, more out of hope than anything else. 'It's never been anything too serious.'

'Well let us know what happens, OK?'

'Yeah, bye, mate.'

I thought for a moment about the dog. Miffy. I guess no matter how much Rube and I complained about him, we knew we'd sort of miss him if something happened to him. It's funny how there are things in this world that do nothing but annoy you, but you know you'd miss them when they're gone. Miffy, the Pomeranian wonder-dog, was one such thing.

Later, when I was sitting in the lounge room with Rube, I missed many opportunities to tell him about Octavia and me.

Now, I told myself. *Now!*

No words ever came out, though, and we just sat there.

The next night I went up and paid Steve a visit. It had been a while since I'd been to see him, and in a way, I missed him. It's hard to pinpoint exactly what it was, but I'd grown to like Steve's company a lot, even though very little was ever said. Sure, we spoke more than we used to, but it still wasn't much.

When I got there only Sal was home.

'He should be here any minute,' she said, in a not-too-thrilled voice. 'You want something to eat? Drink?'

'Nah. I'll be right.'

She didn't make me feel too welcome that night, like she just wasn't up to tolerating me this time around. Her expression seemed to throw words down to me. Words like:

Loser.

Dirty little bastard.

I'm sure that at some point, a while ago, before Steve and I gathered an understanding of each other, he probably told Sal what a couple of loserous bastards he was the brother of. He'd always looked down on Rube and me when we all lived together. We did stupid things, I admit it: stealing road signs, fighting, gambling at the dog track . . . It wasn't quite Steve's scene.

When he came in, about ten minutes later, he actually smiled and said, 'Hey, I haven't seen you for a while!' For a moment, I smiled back and thought he was talking to me, before realizing it was Sal he was talking to. She'd been doing a lot of interstate work lately. He walked over and kissed her. Then he noticed his brother sitting on the couch.

'Hey Cam.'

'Hi Steve.'

I could see they wanted to be alone, so I waited a few seconds and stood up. The kitchen light surrounded them in the dimly lit lounge room.

'Hey, I'll come back some other time,' I said too fast. I made sure to get the hell out of there. Sal was giving me the best *piss off* look I'd ever seen.

'No.'

I was just about out the door when the word booted itself into my back. I turned round and Steve was standing behind me. His face was serious as he spoke the rest of the words.

'You don't have to go, Cam.'

All I did was look at my brother and say, 'Don't worry,' and I turned and left without thinking too much about it. I had other places to go now anyway.

It was still fairly early, so I decided to run to the station and get a train down to Hurstville. In the train's window I saw my reflection – my hair was getting longer again and standing up wild and rough. It was black. Pitch-black in the window, and for the first time, I kind of liked it. Swaying with the train, I looked inside me.

Octavia's street was wrapped in darkness. The lights from the houses were like torchlights. If I closed my eyes tight and opened them again, it looked like the houses were stumbling around in the dark, finding their way. At any moment I expected them to fade. Sometimes human shadows crossed through them, as I waited, just outside her front gate.

For a while, I imagined myself walking to the front door and knocking, but I stayed patient. For some reason, it didn't seem right to go in. Not yet. I was dying for her to come out, make no mistake about that. Yet I knew that if I had to leave again without even a glimpse of her, I would. If I could do it for a girl who cared nothing for me, I could do it for Octavia.

In that one stolen second, I considered the Glebe girl. She entered my mind like a burglar, then vanished gain, taking nothing. It was like the humiliation of the past had been taken instantly from my back and left somewhere on the ground. I wondered for a moment how I could stand outside her house so many times. I even laughed. At myself. She was erased completely a few minutes later when Octavia moved the kitchen curtain aside, and came out to meet me.

The first thing I noticed, before any words hit the air, was the shell. It was tied to a piece of string and was hanging around her neck.

'It looks good.' I nodded, and I reached out and held it in my right hand.

'It does,' she agreed.

We went to the same park as the first night I came, but this time we didn't sit on the splintered bench. This time we walked over the dewy grass and ended up stopping by an old tree.

'Here,' I said, and I gave Octavia the words I wrote the previous night in bed. 'They're yours.'

She read them and kissed the paper and held onto me for quite a while. I told her I loved the howling sound of her harmonica. That seemed to be the limit of my courage that night. I had to get back home, so I couldn't stay too long. It was just nice to see her and touch her and give her the words.

When we made it back to the gate, I kissed her hand and left.

'See you this weekend?' she asked.

'Definitely.'

'I'll call you,' she said, and I was on my way.

At my place, when I returned, I was shocked to find Steve on our front porch, waiting for me.

'I was wondering how long I'd have to sit here,' he fired when I showed up. 'I've been here an hour.'

I walked closer. 'And? Why'd you come?'

'Come on,' he said, standing up. 'Let's go back up to my place.'

'I'll just go in and—'

'I already told 'em.'

Steve's car was parked farther along the street, and after getting in, there were very few words spoken in the car. I turned the radio up but don't remember the song.

'So what's this all about?' I asked. I looked at him but Steve's eyes were firmly on the road. For a while I was wondering if he'd even heard my question. He let his eyes examine me for a second or two, but he said nothing. He was still waiting.

When we got out of the car, he said, 'I want you to meet someone.' He slammed the door. 'Or actually, I want her to meet you.'

We walked up the stairs and into his apartment. It was empty.

'Looks like she's in the shower,' he mentioned. He stood and made coffee and put a cup down in front of me. It still swirled, taking my reflection with it. Taking me down.

For a moment, I thought we were about to go through our usual routine of questions and answers about everyone back at home, but I could see him deciding not to do it. He'd been at our place earlier and found out for himself. It wasn't in Steve's nature to manufacture conversation.

I hadn't been to watch him at football for a while, so I asked how it was going. He was in the middle of explaining it when Sal came out of the bathroom, still drying her hair.

'Hey,' she said to me.

I nodded, giving her half a smile.

That was when Steve stood up and looked at me, then at her. I knew right then that at some point, like I'd expected, he did tell her about Rube and me. I'd imagined it on the park bench in Hurstville for some reason, and I could hear the quiet tone of Steve's intense voice practically disowning his brothers. Now he was rewriting it, or at least trying to make it right.

'Stand up,' he told me.

I did.

He said, 'Sal.' She looked at me. I looked at her, as Steve kept talking. 'This is my brother Cameron.'

We shook hands.

My boyish, rough hand.

Her smooth and clean hand, which smelled of perfumed soap. Soap I imagined you'd get in hotel rooms I'd never get to visit.

She recognized me through the eyes and I was Cameron now, not just that loser brother of Steve.

On the way back home sometime after that, Steve and I talked a while, but only about small things. In the middle of it, I cut him short. I said, with knifelike words, 'When you first told Sal about Rube and me you said we were losers. You told her you were ashamed of us, didn't you?' My voice was still calm and not even the slightest bit accusing, though I was trying as hard as I could.

'No.' He denied it when the car came to a stop outside our house.

'No?' I could see the shame in his eyes, and for the first time ever, I could see it was shame he held for himself.

'No,' he confirmed, and he looked at me with something that resembled anger now, almost like he couldn't stomach it. 'Not you and Rube,' he explained, and his face looked injured. 'Just you.'

God.

God, I thought, and my mouth was open. It was as if Steve had reached into me and pulled out my pulse. My heart was in his hands and he was staring down at it, as if he too could see it.

Beating.

Thrusting itself down, then standing up again. Almost bleeding down his forearms.

I said nothing about the truth Steve had just let loose.

All I did was undo my seat belt, take my heart, and get out of the car as fast as I could.

Steve followed but it was too late. I heard his footsteps coming after me when I was walking onto our porch. Words fell down between his feet.

'Cam!' he called out. 'Cameron!' I was nearly inside when I heard his voice cry out. 'I'm sorry, I was . . .' He made his voice go louder. 'Cam, I was wrong!'

I got behind the door and shut it, then turned to look back out.

Steve's figure was shadowed onto the front window. It was silent and still, plastered to the light.

'I was wrong.'

He said it again, though this time his voice was weaker.

A minute shuddered past.

I broke.

Walking slowly to the front door, I opened it and saw my brother on the other side of the flyscreen.

I waited, then, 'Forget about it,' I said. 'It doesn't matter.'

I was still hurt, but like I said, it didn't matter. I'd been hurt before and I'd be hurt again. Steve must have wished he'd never tried showing Sal that I wasn't the loser she thought I was. All he'd succeeded in doing was proving that not only had he once thought I *was* a lost cause, but that I was the *only* one.

Soon, though, I was stabbed.

The feeling shook through me and cut me loose. All my thoughts were off the chain, until one solitary sentence arrived and wouldn't leave me.

The words and Octavia.

That was the sentence.

It wavered in me.

It saved me, and almost whispering, I said to Steve, 'Don't worry, brother. I don't need you to tell Sal that I'm not a loser.' We were still separated by the flyscreen. 'I don't need you to say it to *me* either. I know what I am. I know what I see. Maybe one day I'll tell you a little more about me, but for now, I guess we'll just have to wait and see what happens. I'm nowhere near what I'm going to be, and . . .' I could feel something in me. Something I've always felt. I paused and caught his eyes. I leaped into them through the door and held him down. 'You ever hear a dog cry, Steve? You know, howling so loud, it's almost unbearable?' He nodded. 'I reckon they howl like that because they're so hungry it hurts, and that's what I feel in me every day of my life. I'm so hungry to be somethin' – to be *somebody*. You hear me?' He did. 'I'm not lyin' down ever. Not for you. Not for anyone.' I ended it. 'I'm hungry, Steve.'

Sometimes I think they're the best words I've ever said.

'I'm hungry.'

And after that, I shut the door.

I didn't slam it.

You don't shoot a dog when it's already dead.

WHEN DOGS CRY

I saw a dog cry once.

It was one of those nights when the wind tries to tear the ground along with it, and a storm stirs itself amongst the sky. Lightning roared and thunder cracked above me.

The street was empty but for the dog, first walking the dangerous, desolate city floor, silently clicking over it with his paws and claws. He looked hungry, and desperate, until he simply stood there, and began.

He reached deep, and his fur stood on end, climbing ferociously up. From his heart, from everything in his instinct, he began to howl.

He howled above the howling thunder. He howled above

the howling lightning, and beyond the howling wind.

With his head claiming the endless sky, he howled hunger and I felt it rise through me.

It was my hunger.

My pride.

And I smiled.

Even now, I smile, and I feel it in my eyes, because hunger's a powerful thing.

13

The phone was ringing. Wednesday night. Just past seven o'clock.

'Hello?'

'Ruben Wolfe?'

'No, it's Cameron here.'

'Tell you what,' the voice went on, laced with friendly malice. 'Could you get him for me?'

'Yeah, who's callin'?'

'No one.'

'No one?'

'Listen, mate. Just get y' brother on the phone or we'll beat the crap out of you as well.'

I was taken aback. I pulled the phone away, then returned it to my ear. 'I'll get him. Hang on a minute.'

Rube was in our room with Julia the Scrubber. I knocked on the door and went in.

'What?' said Rube. He wasn't happy to see me, and neither was Julia. She adjusted her clothing.

I took another step into the room. 'Someone on the phone.'

'For me?' Rube asked.

I nodded.

'Well, who is it?'

'Do I look like y' bloody secretary? Just get up and answer the phone.'

He looked strangely at me, got up grudgingly, and walked out, which left me in the room with Julia the Scrubber, alone.

Julia the Scrubber: 'Hi Cam.'

Me: 'Hi Julia.'

Julia the Scrubber, smiling and moving closer: 'Rube's been tellin' me you're not too much in love with me.'

Me, inching away: 'Well, I guess he can tell you whatever he wants.'

Julia the Scrubber, sensing my complete lack of interest: 'Is it true?'

Me: 'Well, I don't know, to be honest. It isn't really any of my business what Rube does . . . but I know for sure that whoever's on that phone wants to kill him, and I've got some idea it's because of you.'

Julia the Scrubber, laughing: 'Rube's a big boy. He can take care of himself.'

Me: 'That's true, but he's also my brother, and there's no way I'd let him bleed alone.'

Julia the Scrubber: 'How very noble of you.'

Rube came back in, saying, 'I don't know what you're talkin' about, Cam. There's no one on the phone.'

'I'm tellin' you,' I said, pulling Rube out into the hallway. Once we got there, I whispered at him. 'There was a guy there, Rube, and he sounded like he wanted to kill you. So when the phone rings again, get up and answer it.'

The phone did ring again and this time Rube came running out of the room and got it. Again, they hung up on him. By the third time, Rube barked into the phone. 'How 'bout you start talkin'? If you want Ruben Wolfe, you've got him. So talk!'

There was no response from the other end, and the phone didn't ring again that night, but after Julia left, I could see that Rube was a little pensive. He was about as worried as Ruben Wolfe gets, because he knew without doubt now, like I did, that something was coming. In our room, he looked at me. In the exchanging of our eyes, he was telling me a fight was looming.

He sat on his bed.

'I guess that bad feeling you had was right,' he began. 'About Julia. It's definitely that last bloke she had.' It wasn't like Rube to be scared, because we both knew he could take care of himself. He was one of the most liked but most feared people in our neighbourhood. The only trouble now was that nothing was certain. It was a feeling, that's all, and I could sense Rube was feeling it as well. I could smell it.

'Did you ask what's-her-name about him?'

'Julia?'

'Yeah.'

'She reckons he isn't the brightest spark, and that he's got way too much time and a lot of friends. She was with him for about a year.'

'And she just up and ditched him?'

Rube looked over. 'That would about cover it.'

'For you? He must be a real ugly bastard if she quit him for *you*.'

'Don't get smart,' he half warned. 'I'd consider getting after him, but you always end up worse when you do that. That's when they come back for y' with half their bloody neighbourhood behind 'em.'

We were quiet for a while, both thinking about it.

'If somethin' comes up,' I finally said, 'I'll be there, OK?'

Rube nodded. 'Thanks, brother.'

The phone rang the next night as well, and the next.

On the third call of Friday night, Rube picked up the phone and shouted, 'What!?'

He then grew quiet.

'Yeah.' A pause. 'Yeah, sorry about that.' He looked over at me and shrugged his shoulders. 'I'll get him.' He took the receiver away and covered the mouthpiece. 'It's for you.' He held it out to me, thinking. What was he thinking?

'Hello?'

'It's me,' she said. Her voice reached through the phone and took me. 'You working tomorrow?'

'Till about four-thirty.'

She thought for a moment. 'Maybe,' she said, 'we can do something when you get back. I know an old movie house. I think they're playing *Raging Bull*.' Her words were soft but intense. The voice was excitement. The voice was shivers.

I smiled. I couldn't help it. 'For sure.'

'I'll come over just after four-thirty.'

'Good, I'll see you then.'

'I have to go.' She almost cut me off, and she didn't say goodbye. She said, 'I'm watching the clock,' and she was gone.

When I hung up, Rube asked what I knew he would.

'Who was that?' He bit into an apple. 'She sounded familiar.'

I moved closer and sat at the kitchen table and swallowed. I concentrated on breathing. This was it. This was it and I had to say it. 'Remember Octavia?'

Nothing was said.

The tap dripped.

It exploded into the sink.

Rube was halfway through another bite when he realized what I was saying.

His head tilted. He swallowed the piece of apple and made the calculation, while I was thinking, *Oh no, what the hell's about to happen here?*

Something happened.

It happened when Rube went and tightened the tap, turned back round, and said, 'Well, Cam . . .' He laughed.

Was that a good laugh or a bad one? Good laugh, bad laugh? Good laugh, bad laugh? I couldn't decide. I waited.

'What?' I asked. I couldn't stand it any more.

'Tell me.'

Nervously, I started telling him about what happened. I told him about standing outside the house in Glebe. About Octavia showing up. About the train and going there, and the shell, and—

'It's all right, Cam,' he said, but I wasn't sure about the expression on his face. 'That Octavia,' and he shook his head now. 'You'll treat her like a goddess, won't y', Cam?'

I smiled, but didn't bare my teeth. This seemed too easy.

He repeated the question. 'Won't y', Cam?' because we both knew the answer.

This time, I couldn't hide the smile, even though I was still uneasy about Rube's response. He *seemed* happy enough, but in all honesty, Rube was never the type to let you wonder what he was thinking. He laughed a little and I decided that was a good thing, and we stayed together in the kitchen, just as Sarah came in.

'What's going on?' she asked. 'What's all this smilin'? It looks like the end of a Scooby bloody Doo episode in here.'

Rube clapped his hands. 'Wait till you hear this,'

he nearly shouted. I don't know – he appeared to be trying too hard. 'Remember Octavia?'

'Of course.'

'Well.' He was more subdued now. 'Looks like you'll be seein' a bit more of her again because—'

'I knew it!' Sarah went through him. She pointed at me. 'I knew there was a girl, you little bastard, and *you* wouldn't tell me anything!' I'd never seen Sarah grin like this. 'Wait!' she said, and maybe thirty seconds later, she came back with her Polaroid camera and took an instant shot of Rube and me, both leaning against the sink.

'Smile again, will y's,' she said, and we did.

We crowded around to watch the picture form, and soon I could make out the rough gatherings of Rube's hair and the outline of my face. The apple was still balancing in Rube's hand and we were standing there, leaning, both in old jeans, Rube in a flanno work shirt, me in my old spray jacket. It appeared to be so right, both our faces imprinted with smiles.

Appeared . . .

Sarah pulled the photo closer to her.

'I love this picture,' she said, without a moment's thought, 'It looks like brothers.'

What brothers should be, I thought, and we all

continued looking at it, as the tap still dripped down, exploding more quietly now, into the sink.

'Give us a look at that,' Rube said, and he snatched the photo from Sarah's hand. Immediately, I could tell. Somehow I knew.

The way he did it.

The way his eyes zeroed in on the photo.

I knew my brother was about to ruin everything.

In the last few minutes, it had been coming, and now it was here. A quiet anger about the situation had reached him completely now. He'd decided that he didn't like this at all. Octavia and Cameron – to Rube, it wasn't right. It didn't sound right. It didn't feel right. In his eyes, I could see it now. He was about to end it, on gut feeling.

He smiled, but suddenly it wasn't genuine any more. It was sarcastic as he said, 'Yes, sister, this sure is a great shot you've produced here.' He showed it to her as if he'd taken it himself. 'It's such a great shot of me and young Scraps here, isn't it?'

Sarah was confused. 'Scraps?' she asked, just as I felt my insides collapse.

'Sure,' my brother laughed, still focused on the photo. I could only just hear his words above the anxiety that boxed me in the ears. 'Sure, sister,' he explained. 'Scraps – I find the girls and Cam picks up the scraps . . .'

I remember Sarah looking over at me then.

With a few sentences, Rube had destroyed me. Weeks later, I found out why he *really* did it, but for now, it seemed like he'd done it only because he was capable – because he was the guy who got the girls in this house, not me. Not Cameron. And especially not with a girl who was once with him.

Defeat opened the kitchen floor at my feet, raising its hands up to pull me down. *Stay calm*, I told myself as I watched Sarah pull the photo back from Rube's hands. A wounded look scattered slowly and painfully across her face, and when she looked back at me, I felt my anger gathering itself together. When it was all there, I climbed up from the defeat and stood before my brother, face-to-face.

I read his expression. It shaped up to me.

'You're a real bastard,' I said. It didn't sound like me, though. I didn't normally have this much aggression in me. 'You know that?'

'Well, just remember that you pick up the scraps of a bastard,' he answered. 'If it wasn't for me you'd have nothing,' and that was it. It was all I needed. I leaped at my brother and tore him down to the floor.

In the background I could hear the shrieks of Sarah. I couldn't even understand her for the electricity in my ears, and too quickly, I could see the plates and cups and forks from the table crash silently to the kitchen floor. Straight away, I was on my back. Rube, the faster, the stronger, had me pinned. Next I saw his fist, close up. It met my face right beneath my eye and everything shook. I thought the ceiling was splitting apart, and just when it all joined up and found its right place again, it burst open as my brother threw his fist into my face many times. His knees burned through my shoulders. His eyes tore into me. And his hair showered into his face as I fell limp and took it now without feeling anything.

'Stop it!' I heard Sarah screaming now. She'd gone out and come running back into the kitchen with a bucket of water. She threw it down just as Rube got off me. The freezing water splashed over me, covering me like a nice, icy blanket. 'Bastard!' she yelled and threw the bucket at Rube. He shrugged it off and walked out.

Just before exiting the room, he pointed his finger at me.

'What the hell's *wrong* with you, anyway?' he said callously. 'You couldn't find anything of your own, could y'?' He laughed. 'Jesus! You don't pick up the girls y' brother once had. It's low! It's screwed up, you bloody freak!' He laughed hard and angry and awful. 'How 'bout I give y' Julia's number when we're done? Would y' like that?' He left then, finally, slamming the front door behind him.

And me?

I was spread out on the kitchen floor.

Bruised. Soaked.

Beaten.

I closed my eyes and opened them again. The whole thing seemed surreal.

Did that really happen? I asked myself, but then the swelling on my face proved it to me, aching and turning over my skin. The disbelief and shock held me down – I'd always been worried about telling him, and now my worst fears had been realized. They were free to trample me.

Slowly, I looked all around.

The kitchen floor was covered with water, broken crockery, and other assorted scraps.

PIECES

Sometimes there only seem to be clouds.

Tonight, the clouds hang above me, sulking in the sky. They watch me write the words. I don't even think they bother to read them.

I imagine myself in a room, where some shattered pieces are strewn on the floor, in front of me.

As I walk towards them, I have no idea what they are, so I approach with trepidation. They seem to be a puzzle, all torn up and thrown apart. They look injured.

I crouch down and begin putting them together, finding each scrap that surrounds my feet.

Gradually, I see the picture form as I put it all together.

Gradually, I see.

These pieces on the ground.

Are made of me.

14

I didn't go out with Octavia the next night.

She showed up right at the time she said she would, but when she saw my face, she knew immediately what had happened. I had a bruise that swelled blue around my eye and slid across my cheekbone. When she came onto the porch, I remember seeing her eyes back away from me. It didn't take long for her body to follow.

There was no hello.

No niceties.

I only stood and wanted to touch her hand, and the girl said, 'Is that . . . ?'

Is that.

All I could do was nod my head in agreement with the question that was cut in half. It was an attempt to ignore the pain of it. *Is that from Rube?* is what she'd really meant to say.

Watching her feet.

I recall it so clearly – watching as her feet backed

down the steps, carrying her towards the gate.

She said, 'I'm sorry, Cam.' Her words winced. 'I'm so sorry – I should have known.' The pain she felt at coming between my brother and me was obvious. It was wringing itself out through her expression. Her face dripped to the ground. What she didn't know was that it wasn't just her that came between Rube and me the previous night. It was everything that was different about us. It was Rube being the winner and me not settling to be the under-dog any more. It was the way he treated girls against the way I *wanted* to treat them. It was me facing the reality that I had lived my whole life not in Rube's shadow, but behind it, not even able to touch it. Yes, it felt like everything.

'Please,' I called out then, afraid that it sounded like a yelp. 'Octavia, don't go.'

But she did.

She shook herself from the gate and walked onto the street. Half a walk. Half a run. There was panic in every footstep, and the sound of each one seemed to erase everything else that had happened before. Her face had been so full of sacrifice. In an instant she was willing to give up whatever she wanted, or what the two of us wanted, for the sake of Rube and me. She left so fast, and my reactions were simply too slow.

Can it be so quick? I asked myself. *Can everything burn down so fast? Can she just tread past me because of Rube?*

The truth of it kept rolling over me. It was like a virus, arriving with more strength with each passing thought of it. I replayed it at least a hundred times within a few minutes. Her words, her face. And the savage sound of her soft, falling footsteps.

How could it be so fast? I asked again, but there were no answers. A week ago she wanted every piece of me. She loved me even for my failures, like not being able to lean on the glass windows in the tower. She loved the shell and my words. All those things were gone now.

I'd envisioned so many things for this night.

A cold street with us walking through it, warm.

An empty movie cinema, but for us.

Laughing.

Talking.

Sitting in the underground waiting for Octavia's train home.

Counting the trains as they pulled in, waited, then pulled back out — we'd be too happy for her to get on a train and go home. I'd sit there, proud that I could make Octavia Ash this happy . . .

It all brushed past me with the icy breeze that lifted itself to our front porch and swept across my face.

A few minutes later, in *real* reality, the door slammed behind me and Rube walked out. We looked at each other a moment, but nothing was said. All day at work, he and I had said nothing to each other. On account of my face, Dad knew we'd fought, but he stayed out of it. We'd fought before and got over it, but this time I wasn't so sure.

As I sat there in the darkness of the porch, Rube only continued down the steps and onto the street, just like Octavia. When he was gone, I realized that neither of them had looked back at me.

The night was cold, but for a long time, I stayed there, enjoying it in a depressed sort of way. The wind grew stronger and slapped me in the face and even my jacket pockets were soaked with bitter coldness.

It was the first night I'd ever gone out with a girl – and I never even made it off the front porch.

Eventually, I went back inside.

I watched TV with Mr and Mrs Wolfe but I saw

and heard nothing. When they laughed at something, it shocked me.

Soon after, I went into Rube's and my room and sat against the wall, under the window. In the dark. It's unfortunate to admit, but some tears burned their way down my face. When there was a knock at the door, I didn't even bother wiping them off.

I said nothing.

Another knock, but this time, Sarah walked in and hit the light. I let the pain of it ignite in my eyes.

'You didn't go out?' she asked.

Slowly, I shook my head.

'Why not?'

'She saw my face.' My voice was numb. 'And she knew Rube and I had fought.'

'And that's it? She just left.'

'She ran,' I pointed out.

'I see . . .'

There was a while of no talking then, but Sarah sat down at the opposite end of the room from me. We only sat there, staring, and I must admit that it was kind of nice to have some company. When she got up, she came over and offered me a hand.

'Come on,' she said. 'Let me show you something.'

Cautiously, I took it and stood up, following her

out of the room, down the hall, and into her own room.

'Shut the door,' she said.

I did as I was told.

She lifted her mattress and pulled out a big spiral booklet. Some Polaroids fell out. I noticed the one with Rube and me in the kitchen, right before the fight.

'Sit down.'

Again, I did as I was told, and before my eyes, I saw the secret life of Sarah Wolfe, my sister. She turned pages and on each sheet, there was a sketch or a drawing, or a fully realized charcoal-coloured work. There were sketches of our house, our family, our street. There were mothers dragging kids along at the supermarket, people boarding trains, cars lined up like dominoes on Elizabeth Street, and leftovers heating up in the kitchen.

She gave me the book and I kept turning the pages, looking down in awe at the strength and feeling in the drawings.

There was Dad getting out of his panel van after work.

Mrs Wolfe sleeping on the couch one night, exhausted.

An anonymous person struggling down the street in the rain.

Page after page.

It took me a few minutes to be able to speak.

'They're brilliant,' I said.

'Just keep going.' She nodded. 'Go to page thirty-eight.'

I turned all the pages until I found the right one.

Standing on that page was me. I was standing there in coloured charcoal, in a blue suit, with a red tie, black shoes. My face was dirty but my head was high, and of course, my hair was a shocker – all tangled and rough and reaching for the sky. Most importantly, though, I was wearing a pair of red boxing gloves.

Cameron Wolfe.

In a blue suit and boxing gloves . . .

'I love it,' I said to my sister.

'Yes,' she said, 'but do you know what it means, Cameron?' Any form of a smile left her face. She was serious. 'Should I tell you what it means?'

'The suit and the gloves?'

'Yes.'

I looked straight at her. 'Tell me.'

She answered. 'Well, first of all, you're dirty.

That's what you've always considered yourself to be – dirty, small, not worth much.' She pointed now to the suit. 'The suit tells us that you've had enough of that. You want so badly to be better that it hurts . . . am I right?'

Dumbly, I nodded.

'Then, the gloves.' She was strong, and so sure. 'The gloves show that you'll always fight to get there, to be that person.' Now she became even more determined, and her words ran at me. Into me. 'But I'll tell you something, Cam – if you still want that girl and leave things as they are . . . if you just let that girl walk away, I'll rub those gloves off altogether and disfigure your hands. I'll even make it look like you're about to cut them off.' Her last words were spoken harshly. 'You got it?'

Silently, I agreed.

'Do you still want her?' she said.

'Of course.' There was no other answer.

'Well, don't,' she continued, 'let Rube, or anyone else tell you what to do or what to be. Don't worry about what everyone else wants, just so their own miserable lives can be easier. Do what *you* want, Cam. Understand?'

For the last time, I nodded.

'Now shut the door behind you.' This time she smiled.

I walked to the door but turned round halfway and returned to my sister. I leaned down quickly and kissed her cheek, then walked back out.

'Hey Cam,' she called, just before I was gone. I turned back. 'And keep writing too . . .'

I stepped closer. 'How did . . . ?

I gave up and nodded, and walked back up the hall.

THE HALLWAY

If there are alleys inside me, there must also be hallways.

I take a walk inside, treading past rooms and closets, to find a dark hallway where I've never been before. There's no door, so I walk right in, find a string, and pull on it, to produce the adequate light.

The hallway glows now, but dimly enough to not hurt my eyes.

Slowly, I look from side to side as I walk, and I understand that this is a hallway of underdogs.

Plastered to the walls are the images of Sarah Wolfe, my sister. They're the photos and drawings from her notebook — the people on the street, my mother and father, the ones struggling with their shopping. They're all people fighting their way through their lives.

I study each one on my way through.

They keep me, and I keep them.

. . . At the end of the hallway, there's a light. It's a lot brighter than what's in here, but it blinks. It even seems to be limping in its attempt to get my attention.

I keep walking, towards that limping light. I vow to remember each person I've just seen, each image of the hallway.

The light awaits me, and I approach it, uncertain.

15

After everything that had happened, there was no chance of sleeping that night. I considered getting myself down to Octavia's place, but decided to wait out the hours and find her the next day down at the harbour.

There was an old movie on TV.

I watched it until I staggered to bed and dropped in.

Earlier, I wrote some words and tucked them under my mattress, and lying in bed, they seemed to crawl out and step over me as I stared at the ceiling.

It was late when Rube came in, tired and clumsy. He tripped over his shoes after he swept them off his feet, and briefly, before he went to bed, he came and stood over me. With my eyes closed, I could feel the presence of my brother.

Keep your eyes shut, I told myself. I came close to saying something to him, but I remembered the kitchen and the fight, and the words and the fists. A hatred climbed into bed with me, whispering that I should be still and silent and wait for the intruder to leave.

The intruder.

It hurt to think of my brother like that, but in one glorious moment, he had ripped apart the first chance I ever had.

To touch a girl.

To be with a girl . . .

'Hey Scraps,' I imagined him saying, but he said nothing.

He only stood there.

Even now, I wonder what he was thinking at that moment.

Was he contemplating throwing his hand down to wake me, to call me brother and say he was sorry? Or did he want to ask me why I couldn't find a girl of my own? Did he want to plead with me to stop being his shadow?

I'll never know, because the moment passed and never came up again. It ended when his feet dragged him over to his own bed and he fell down, on top of the sheets. It seemed fitting that night that Rube rarely covered himself in bed. He didn't need the warmth, whereas I froze if I wasn't covered up to my nose, lying there with just my snout sticking up for air.

The hours dragged themselves by, and when Rube began to snore it felt like insult being lent to injury. The sound tore open the night, as I lay there with visions swimming and circling in my head. It was mostly Octavia, but images of Rube and Steve and Sarah also made their way inside me. I kept seeing the drawing Sarah showed me – the blue suit and the boxing gloves. For some reason, the visions of Steve also bothered me. I kept hearing the words he'd spoken – it was funny how my two brothers were so capable of hurting me, and how my sister was the one who could see something in me to believe in. All this time, she'd been watching, and I guess, if it wasn't for her, I wouldn't have resolved that night to find Octavia the next day, and to face Steve one last time.

In the morning, I decided Steve would be first.

Around ten, I walked up to his apartment. I didn't have to ring the buzzer because he and Sal were up on the balcony. He didn't call me up. Instead, he disappeared and came down to meet me. It was a gesture, I guess. He was coming to me.

He opened his mouth to speak, but I beat him.

'Where you on at today?' My voice was friendly. Giving.

Steve looked up at the balcony, but he didn't answer my question. He said, 'What are you doing here?' I could tell he was shocked that I'd come, to face him in daylight. 'If I were you, I'd never speak to me again.' He looked away. 'If I were you, I'd hate me for ever.'

'But I'm *not* you,' I said. 'I can't beat up a group of guys one by one. I can't kick a goal after beer's been thrown at my head – hell, I can't even kick one *without* the beer. But I *can* stand here, in front of you. I can look you in your eyes when you never expected to see me again. I can survive anything you do or say to me.'

The breeze took a breath.

It paused – stopped completely – and Steve spoke. 'OK.'

For a last moment, I looked at him, then left. I moved out from under the balconies and called up to Sal, 'I'll see y' later,' then turned back to Steve. 'I might come up tomorrow or later in the week. Maybe we can go up to the oval.'

'Sounds good,' he replied, and we went our own ways.

That was the first part done. Now for Octavia.

I went by train to the harbour, and when I stepped out onto the platform, I felt like nothing today would stop me. All my thoughts leaned now towards the girl, and from the railing, I looked for the crowd of people that would be gathered around her, watching, listening, and taking in the music that flowed from her.

She wasn't there, though.

The place that was hers was completely empty. Not even other buskers went there, because it seemed Octavia had ownership of it. The stretch towards the Harbour Bridge was only that — a stretch, a path. There was no music, and no people.

I ran down there and stood alone at the exact place, hit hard by the silence that surrounded me. For a few minutes, I looked wildly around, trying to find something, anything that would lead me to a scent of the girl.

Nothing.

I even asked some people if they'd seen a harmonica player.

They said there was one over the other side, near the Opera House, and barely remembering to thank them, I took off. I ran round to the other side, past the ferry entrance, the ticket offices, and the boulevard of too-expensive cafés and restaurants.

Finally, near the Opera House steps, I could hear the sound of a harmonica and hoped.

There! I thought, but when I rounded the corner, there was an old man, sitting down, playing. No Octavia.

My hopes struggled forward.

They fell crooked as I moved in a staggered circle, looking and attempting to find her. I began walking the city, and soon realized that I'd be walking all afternoon. My feet took me through the entire city centre, but all I found were those mime people, pen sellers for the Royal Blind Society, and the odd didgeridoo player. The girl was nowhere.

With aching legs and feet, I eventually boarded a train for Hurstville and walked back down to Octavia's place. God, it was such a parody of the first time I'd walked down there. The nerves were even more intense now, but the reality was awful. It was almost obscene, because last time, I knew she wanted me. Deep down, I knew. This time, though, if she was in there, I couldn't be sure if she would come out. And even if she did, would it be to tell me to go home, go away, go anywhere as long as it was away from her?

It was late afternoon when I made it there and started the vigil.

Soon, an hour was gone and so was the light.

The streetlights scratched themselves on.

There was no Octavia.

There was no girl.

There was only me, Cameron Wolfe, standing in front of a house where Octavia Ash happened to live. At one point, there was movement near the light that hid behind the front door, but no one came out.

You better go, I told myself, but not before I stayed one last minute and reminded myself of what this all meant. The cruelty of it walked past, digging its shoulder into me along the way. *The cruelty*, I thought, because here I was again, standing outside a girl's house who didn't want me – and this time it was worse, much worse, because she'd even asked me to stand there. Only twenty-four hours ago, she'd still wanted me, and now, it was all finished. I was still alone. I was still standing there, and now it wasn't just a walk from home. Now I had to come a lot further to stand amongst the same failure, to feel the same aloneness and humiliation.

When I left, I looked back, and there was no one looking out the window or brushing a curtain aside to watch me leave. There was nothing but the empty street and me.

The next night was the same.

Then, the next, and the next.

I resolved to stand there every night until Octavia came out, no matter how long it took.

It became routine, like waking up and putting on your pants. My routine was getting up, walking to school, and contemplating all of it as I stared at graffitied desks and wandered through the lonely halls of each building. I noticed how much laughter there was at school. It came to me suddenly, like echoes, like paint. Like paint splayed over me, colouring me a sickly human colour. I would do what had to be done there, then head down to Octavia's, stand for two hours, and come home. Dinner was next, and walking Miffy, alone. Rube stopped walking him with me after the fight.

It was rare for me to see Rube at all that week.

The only time we spoke was when the phone started ringing again.

'It's the Phonecaller,' I'd tell him. I never hung

around to listen to what was said, and most times the phone was left dead. I could see Rube getting more and more frustrated, and I quietly felt glad that his womanizing had made his life at least a little uncomfortable.

As for the vigils down in Hurstville, the door finally opened on Friday night, but it wasn't Octavia who came out. It was a woman who had clearly given Octavia the shape of her face, and her eyes and lips. She walked slowly, almost sadly towards me.

There was kindness in her eyes and I recall the sincerity in her voice.

When she was close enough, she said, 'You're Cameron, aren't you?'

I nodded. 'Yes, Mrs Ash, I am.' I kept my head up and made sure to look at her. *Keep proud*, I thought.

'I thought it best to come out and tell you that Octavia's not here tonight – she's gone to stay at a friend's place for the weekend.' I could tell it pained her slightly to have to speak to me like this. 'You should go home.'

'OK.'

I said the word but I didn't mean it.

Nothing was OK, and I didn't want to go home.

Before I walked away, I turned and asked, 'The whole weekend?'

Mrs Ash nodded. 'Take tomorrow night off – you deserve a rest.' Her eyes swayed momentarily. 'And Cameron?'

'Yes.'

'For what it's worth, I'm sorry, OK?'

That was when I simply stood there, I didn't want her pity. I wanted to spit at it. Throw it off me. Kill it. Yet all I managed to do was stand there a few seconds more and walk away.

I'll be back Sunday, I said to myself when I turned off the street, and I wondered if the girl truly was at a friend's place.

'You haven't given up, have you?' Sarah asked me the next night, and I told her about the conversation with Mrs Ash. We were in her room. Her photos and some other small drawings were sitting on the desk.

'Don't worry,' I reassured her. 'I'll be back there tomorrow night.'

'Good.'

Like clockwork, I was there again the next night, and then every evening during the week. I stood there for up to two hours. Sometimes longer. A few times, it looked like rain, but it didn't come until a week and a half later. I stood there and splinters of rain soon turned to nails. I remained standing there, soaked, and that was what finally drew the girl out the front door and onto the porch.

'Cameron!?' she cried out, and I begged for her next words to be, 'Come inside, come inside,' but they weren't.

She came down towards the gate and the rain clamped down on her hair and dribbled down her face. Her voice was hard and loud, and it trapped me amongst the rain.

'Cameron, get out of here!' it was almost a shriek. Her green eyes were desperate and full of warm water, ready to mix with the ice that seemed to be bucketing from the sky. It didn't even take a minute for her to be completely wet and she was so beautiful, it nearly made me choke. 'Go!' she shouted again. 'Go home!' She closed her eyes in pain and turned, to go back inside.

She was nearly at the front door when I found my voice. It made its way over my beating heart and into my mouth.

'Why!?' I called to her. She turned to face me as I went on. 'Why are you doing this to me!?' I swallowed, and met her face. 'You rescued me from this once. Why are you putting me through it again?'

Hurt, she moved to the edge of the steps, raised her head, and punctured me.

She said, 'Well maybe it's time you started rescuing yourself!'

It rained – harder and louder – and we stood there, each alone, as the words defeated both of us. Octavia was wounded and wet, and slowly, completely soaked with sorrow, she turned and went back inside. I remained at the gate, crushed by the heaviness of her words and the rain.

In the train on the way home, no one sat next to me because I was so wet.

There was so much of me, drooling all over the seat and onto the floor, sitting in a pool of defeat. At Central, I pulled my ticket out of my pocket, but all that was left of it was a soggy lump of paper. It would never go through the machine.

A collector was in the booth. She was a relatively old lady with some facial hair, and she was chewing gum. When I approached her, I held out the pathetic clump in my hand.

'*That's* your ticket?' she enquired.

'That's right,' I answered morosely.

She studied me for a second or two but decided

to let me through. 'One of those days, huh?'

'Shocker,' I answered, and she winked at me on my way past.

'Don't worry, love,' she chewed. 'Things can only get better from here.' To that, I said nothing. I only listened as my soaked shoes squeaked on the dirty tile floor, and I imagined the trail of wet footprints stretching out behind me. It felt like those footprints stretched back for ever.

IF HER SOUL SHOULD LEAK

I'm running, with wet feet.

There's a girl up ahead.

She doesn't move fast, but no matter how hard I run, I can't catch up with her. My feet become heavier and more sodden with every step. I want to call out, but somehow I know she won't hear.

Even as other people pass by, I want to tell them. I want to say it —

I love that girl.

But I don't.

Eventually, she turns a corner and by the time I make it round, she's gone.

Defeated, I lean back to the cold, hard bricks, and I

understand that there are many things I haven't seen or felt or known.

At this moment, there's only one thing I know for sure.

It's about the girl, and it's this.

If her soul ever leaks, I want it to land on me.

16

It rained nonstop for a week, and amongst all the water, an event occurred that had the potential to turn everything on its head.

A tragedy.

A debacle.

And you guessed it, it involves Miffy, the wonder-dog, the little bastard, the ball of fluff who's always managed to elbow his way into our lives.

What happened was this:

The poor little guy just up and died on us.

It was Thursday afternoon and torrential rain poured itself down, battering the streets and rooftops. Someone was smashing their fist into our front door.

'Hang on!' I yelled. I was glumly eating toast in the lounge room.

I opened the door and there was a small balding man on his knees, completely drenched.

'Keith?' I asked.

He looked up at me. I dropped the toast. Rube was behind me now, asking, 'What's goin' on?'

Keith's face was covered in sorrow. Dribbles of rain ambled down his face as he slowly picked himself up. He fixed his eyes on our kitchen window and said it, with pain rinsing through his voice.

'Miffy.' He almost went to pieces again. 'He's dead. In the back yard.'

Rube and I looked at each other.

We ran out the back and clambered over the fence as the back door slammed behind us. Halfway over the fence, I saw it. There was a soggy ball of fluff lying motionless amongst the grass.

No, I thought, as I landed on the other side. Disbelief held me down inside my footsteps, making my body heavy but my thoughts wild.

Rube also hit the ground. His feet slapped down into the sodden grass, and where my footsteps ended, his began.

I kneeled down in the pouring rain.

The dog was dead.

I touched him.

The dog was dead.

I turned to Rube, who was kneeling next to me. For the moment, our differences were cast aside.

The dog was dead.

We sat there a while, completely silent as the rain fell like needles onto our soaked bodies. The fluffy brown fur of Miffy the pain-in-the-arse Pomeranian was being dented by the rain, but it was still soft, and clammy. Both Rube and I stroked him. A few stray tears even sprang into my eyes. I recalled all the times we walked him at night with smoke climbing from our lungs and with laughter in our voices. I heard us complaining about him, ridiculing him, but deep down, caring for him. *Even loving him*, I thought.

Rube's face was devastated.

'Poor little bastard,' he said. His voice clung strangely to his mouth.

I wanted to say something but was completely speechless. I'd always known this day would come, but I didn't imagine it like this. Not pouring rain. Not a pathetic frozen lump of fur, or a feeling as despondent as the one I felt at this exact moment.

Rube picked him up and carried him under the shelter of Keith's back veranda.

The dog was dead.

Even once the rain stopped, the feeling inside me didn't subside. We kept patting him. Rube even apologized to him, probably for all the verbal abuse he'd levelled at him almost every time he saw him.

'Sorry,' he said, and I had to check who he was talking to.

Keith arrived after a while, but it was mainly Rube and me who stayed. For about an hour or so, we sat with him.

'He's getting stiff,' I pointed out at one stage.

'I know,' Rube replied, and I'd be lying if I didn't say a smirk didn't cross our faces. It was the situation, I guess. We were cold, soaking wet, and hungry, and in a way, this was Miffy's final revenge on us – guilt. Or was it a sacrifice, to bring us back together?

Here we were, just about frozen in our neighbour's back yard, patting a dog that was getting stiffer and stiffer by the minute, all because we'd consistently insulted him and then had the audacity to love him.

'Well, forget this,' Rube finally said. He gave Miffy a last pat and told the truth with a wavering voice. He said, 'Miffy – you were undoubtedly a pathetic individual. I hated you, loved you, and wore a hood on my head so no one saw me with you. It's been a pleasure.' He gave him a final pat, on the dog's head. 'Now, I'm leavin',' he pointed out. 'Just because you had the nerve to die under your clothesline in the middle of what was practically a hurricane, I'm not about to get pneumonia because of it. So goodbye – and let's pray the next dog Keith and his wife decide to get is actually a *dog* and not a ferret, rat or rodent in disguise. Goodbye.'

He walked away, into the darkness of the back yard, but as he climbed the fence, he turned and gave Miffy one last look. One last goodbye. Then he was gone. For a moment, I realized that this was more than he'd given me when I sat on the porch that night after Octavia ran from me. He sure as hell didn't look back at *me*. But then, to be fair, I wasn't dead.

I hung around a little while longer, and when Keith's wife came home from work she was quite distressed about what I was beginning to call 'The Miffy Incident'. She kept repeating one thing. 'We'll get him cremated. We've gotta get that dog cremated.' Apparently, Miffy was a gift from her mother, who insisted that all corpses, including her own, had to be burned. 'Gotta get that dog cremated,' she went on, but rarely did she even look at him. Strangely enough, I had the feeling it was Rube and me who loved that dog the most – a dog whose ashes would most likely end up on top of the TV or video, or in the liquor cabinet for safekeeping.

Soon, I said my last goodbye, running my hand over the stiff body and silky fur, still a little shocked by all of it.

I went home and told everyone the news of the cremation. Needless to say, everyone was amazed, especially Rube. Or maybe amazed isn't quite the right word for my brother's reaction. Appalled was more like it.

'Cremate him!' he shouted. He couldn't believe it. 'Did you see that dog!? Did you see how bloody soggy he was!? They'll have to dry him out first or else he'll never even burn! He'll just smoulder! They'll have to get the blow-dryer out!'

I couldn't help but laugh. Trust Rube to still make me laugh despite my hating his guts at that point in time.

It was the blow-dryer, I think.

I kept imagining Keith standing over the poor mongrel with the blow-dryer on full speed and his wife calling out from the back door:

'Is he dry yet, love? Can we chuck him in the fire?'

'No, not yet darlin'!' He'd reply. 'I'll need about another ten minutes, I reckon. I just can't get this damn tail dry!' Miffy had one of the bushiest tails in history of the world. Trust me.

We found out the next day that there'd be a small ceremony on Saturday afternoon at four. The dog was being burned on Friday.

Naturally, as the walkers of Miffy, we were invited next door for the funeral, but it didn't stop there. Keith also decided he wanted to scatter Miffy's ashes in the back yard that was his domain. He asked if we'd like to be the ones who emptied them. 'You know,' he said. 'Since you spent the most time with him.'

'Really?' I asked.

'Well, to be honest' – he shifted on the spot a little – 'the wife wasn't too keen on the idea, but I put my foot down. I said, *No, those boys deserve it and that's it, Norma.*' He laughed and said, 'My wife referred to you as the two dirty bastards from next door.'

Old bitch, I thought.

'Old bitch,' Rube said, but luckily, Keith didn't hear.

On Saturday, Dad, Rube and I finished work at two so we could get home in time for the big funeral, and by four o'clock it was Rube, Sarah and me who went next door. We all climbed the fence.

Keith brought Miffy out in a wooden box, and the

sun was shining, the breeze was curling, and Keith's wife was sneering at Rube and me.

Old bitch, I thought again, and you guessed it, Rube actually said it, as a whisper only he, Sarah and I could hear. It made us all laugh, though I tried to resist. The wife didn't look too happy.

Keith held the box.

He gave a futile speech about how wonderful Miffy was. How loyal. How beautiful. 'And how pitiful,' Rube whispered again, to which I had to bite the inside of my mouth to keep from laughing. A small burst actually made it out, and Keith's wife wasn't too impressed.

Bloody Rube, I thought. Even when I hated him he could make me laugh. Even when I despised everything he stood for and had done to me, he could make me laugh by giving Miffy a good mouthful.

The thing was, though, it was fitting for it to be like this. There was no point in us standing there claiming how much we loved the dog and all that kind of thing. That would only show how much we *didn't* love him. We expressed love for this dog by:

1. Putting him down.
2. Deliberately provoking him.

3. Hurling verbal abuse at him.
4. Discussing whether or not we should throw him over the fence.
5. Giving him meat that was a borderline decision on whether or not he could adequately chew it.
6. Heckling him to make him bark.
7. Pretending we didn't know him in public.
8. Making jokes at his funeral.
9. Comparing him to a rat, ferret, and any other creature resembling a rodent.
10 Knowing without showing that we cared for him.

The problem with this funeral was that Keith was going on and on, and his wife kept insisting on attempting to cry. Eventually, when everyone was bored senseless and almost expecting a hymn to be sung, Keith asked a vital question. In hindsight, I'm sure he wished like hell he didn't ask it at all.

He said, 'Anyone else got something to say?'

Silence.

Then Rube

Keith was just about to hand me the wooden box that contained the last dregs of Miffy the dog when Rube said, 'Actually, yes. I have something to say.'

No, Rube, I thought desperately. *Please. Don't do it.*

But he did.

As Keith handed me the box, Rube made his announcement. In a loud, clear voice, he said, 'Miffy – we will always remember you.' His head was held high. Proud. 'You were strictly the most ridiculous animal on the face of the earth. But we loved you.'

He looked over at Sarah and smiled – but not for long.

Definitely not for long, because before we even had time to think, Keith's wife exploded. She came tearing across at us. She was onto me in a second and she started wrestling me for the bloody box!

'Give us that, y' little bastard,' she hissed.

'What did *I* do?' I asked despairingly, and within an instant there was a war going on with Miffy in the centre of it. Rube's hands were on the box now as well, and with Miffy and me in the middle, he and Norma were going at it. Sarah took some great action shots of the two of them fighting.

'Give us that,' Norma was spitting, but Rube didn't give in. There was no way. They struggled on, Norma with all her might, and Rube in a relaxed, amused way.

In the end, it was Keith who ended it.

He stepped into the middle of the fray and shouted, 'Norma! Norma! Stop being stupid!'

She let go and so did Rube. The only person now with their hands on the box was me, and I couldn't help but laugh at this ridiculous situation. To be honest, I think Norma was still upset about an incident I haven't previously mentioned. It was something that happened two years ago. It was the incident that got us walking Miffy to begin with, when Rube and I and a few other fellas were playing football in our yard. Old Miffy got all excited because of all the noise and the ball constantly hitting the fence. He barked until he had a mild heart attack, and to make up for it, Mrs Wolfe made us pay the vet's bill and take him for walks at least twice a week.

That was the beginning of Miffy and us. The *true* beginning, and although we whinged and carried on about him, we did grow to love him.

In the back yard funeral scene, however, Norma wasn't having any of it. She was still seething. She only calmed down a few minutes later, when we were ready to empty Miffy out into the breeze and the back yard.

'OK Cameron,' Keith nodded. 'It's time.'

He made me stand up on an old lawn chair and I opened the box.

'Goodbye, Miffy,' he said, and I turned the box upside down, expecting Miffy to come pouring out.

The only problem was, he didn't. He was stuck in there.

'Bloody hell!' Rube exclaimed. 'Trust Miffy to be all bloody sticky!'

Keith's wife looked slightly aggravated, to say the least. Actually, I think ropeable would be a more appropriate word.

All I could do was start shaking the box, but still the ashes didn't come out.

'Put your finger in it and stir it round a bit,' Sarah suggested.

Norma looked at her. 'You're not gettin' smart now too, are y', girly?'

'No way,' Sarah replied honestly. Good idea. You wouldn't want to upset this lady at this point in time. She looked about ready to strangle someone.

I turned the box back over and cringed before rummaging my hand through the ashes.

The next time I tried emptying it, there was success. Miffy was set free. As Sarah took the photo, the wind picked up the ashes and scattered them over the yard and into Keith's other neighbour's yard.

'Oh no,' Keith said, scratching his head. 'I knew I should have told next door to take their washing off the line . . .'

His neighbours would be wearing Miffy on their clothes for at least the next couple of days.

PAUSE OF DEATH

I pause a moment and thoughts of death climb onto me. They hang from my shoulders and breathe in my face, and I get to thinking about religion and heaven and hell.

Or to be honest, I think of hell.

There's nothing worse than thinking that that's exactly where you're going when eternity comes for you.

That's where I usually think I'm going.

Sometimes I take comfort in the fact that most people I know are probably going to hell too. I even tell myself that if all my family are going to hell I'd rather go with them than enter heaven. I mean, I'd feel sort of guilty. There they'd be, burning through eternity, while I'm eating peaches and most likely patting pitiful Pomeranians like Miffy up in heaven.

I don't know.

I don't.

Really.

I'm pretty much just hoping to live decent. I hope that's enough.

17

The question now is, what the hell happened next? Every time I think about the whole death of Miffy saga, the story gets obscured in my mind. I have to concentrate to get it right.

The sound.

That's always how I remember – the sound of Rube in the basement, punching the bag that hung in there. He was preparing for the Phonecaller, who was still calling on a three-nights-per-week basis. Rube would stay down there for a long time each night, and when he entered our bedroom, I could see some blood leaking across his knuckles.

If our differences were set aside for Miffy's sake, they returned almost immediately after. In death, Miffy had only brought us together momentarily. He'd failed. There was an outward indifference that Rube constantly sent me in the eyes, if he looked at me at all. The only time he spoke to me was by staring out the window and talking more to himself than to me.

'That friggin' Julia,' he said one night.

It was a cold Tuesday evening at the start of August when Rube got what seemed like the usual call. This time, though, it was Julia. She told him she'd gone back to the previous bloke – the Phonecaller. Apparently he'd begged her to go back and she did. She also warned Rube that he was still after him, to which Rube offered to get it over with immediately, in the back yard, if necessary . . .

The scrubber was gone, but she'd left a legacy.

As he stood at the window and spoke of these things, I remembered once telling him I'd be there if he needed me. 'Thanks, brother.' That's what he'd told me back then, but now I wasn't so sure. I wasn't sure if he would even *want* help from me, and I didn't know if I had the strength to give it to him. I could only watch him at the window, as he enjoyed the hardness of his hands, and the blood that crept from them.

I stopped going to Octavia's place altogether.

'Maybe it's time you started rescuing yourself,' I kept hearing her say, though I could also see the pain on her face. I told myself at times that she didn't mean it; that she didn't want me to stop coming and standing there. She only did it because she thought it was the right thing to do. The irony was that she thought she was keeping Rube and me together by staying away, but as it currently stood, I'd lost both of them.

Days and nights collected up and slipped by, and Rube continued his routine of answering the empty phone calls and blasting the bag in the basement. In a way, I could only feel sorry for someone who wanted to take him on. Even if there were more than one at least a few of them would get hurt, because Rube had speed and strength and no hesitation.

One night when the phone rang I answered it and asked the guy on the other end to hang on. 'My brother wants to talk to you,' I said, 'I mean, this is getting ridiculous. You call three times a week. You say nothing. I'm starting to think you actually *like* my brother rather than want to kill him – otherwise you'd just beat him up and be done with it. So hang on. Just a minute.'

I went down to the basement.

'What is it?'

Rube didn't usually sweat much, but after a good hour on the bag, he was drenched.

'It's him,' I said.

He walked up the cold cement steps and practically mauled the phone when he picked it up.

'Now listen,' he growled. 'I'll be waiting down near the old train yard at eight o'clock tomorrow night. You know where that is? . . . Yeah, that's the one. If you want, come and get me. If not, stop ringin' me – you're a pain in the arse.' There was a longer silence. Rube was listening. 'Good,' he spoke again. 'Just you and me, alone.' Again, he listened. 'That's right – no help, no tricks, and then it's over. Goodbye.' He slammed the phone down and I could see he was already fighting in his mind.

'So it's on?' I asked.

'Apparently so,' and he went to shut the basement door. 'Thank Christ for that.'

Then the phone rang. Again.

Rube picked it up, and immediately, I could tell it was his mate again. Rube wasn't happy.

'What is it this time?' He shot the words through the phone. 'You can't!' He was getting more irritated by the second. 'Now listen, mate – you're the one who wants to kill *me*, so make up your mind about when you feel like doin' it. What about tonight, or right now? No? Well how about Friday?

Could you check your calendar and make sure you've got nothing else on?' He waited. 'Y' sure now? Positive? You won't be ringin' in a minute or two attempting to reschedule? No? So Friday night sounds like a good time to kill me? Good. Same place, same time. *Friday*. Good.'

Again, he hung up, forcefully. He shook his head but laughed. 'It's an absolute circus with this bloke.'

He started eating some bread and got ready to go out. I guess with Julia gone, there were more girls on the horizon. For a moment, I nearly asked if he wanted me to come along on Friday, but I guess he would have viewed that as *scraps* behaviour – following him around.

Anyway, I thought. *He got himself into this*. He'd finally stumbled onto the wrong girl, and maybe he was going to pay. Sure, I also told myself that I'd been wrong in the past, because Rube had often escaped dangerous situations for no other reason than the fact that he was Ruben Wolfe and Ruben Wolfe could handle anything.

With his fists.

With his wayward charm.

Any way he could.

This time, though, I couldn't be sure. It was

different. I guess we'd discover the outcome on Friday night.

There were a few days till then, and I spent most of my time thinking about the confrontation, and Octavia. Always Octavia. I considered writing her a letter or calling her, but I couldn't bring myself to do it. Sarah said I should keep trying.

'You haven't cut my hands off in that picture, have you?' I asked her on Thursday night.

She only shook her head, almost forlornly. 'No, Cam – I think you've fought hard enough. At least for the time being.'

All that was left was Friday night.

Rube got ready in our room at about seven-thirty, putting on his oldest jeans, his work flanno, and boots, which he did up nice and tight. He stared into the mirror, telling himself what to do. Eyeing himself off.

Just before he left, we looked at each other.

What was there to say? Good luck? I hope you get the crap beaten out of you? You want me to come?

No.

It was all silence, and he left.

On his way out, he announced that he was going to a friend's place, shut the door hard, and went out onto the street. Even from the kitchen window, I could tell he was hyped up and hardened. The cold night air seemed to get out of his way as he walked through it.

Now it was decision time.

Was I going after him or not?

The minutes passed and finally I resolved to go. I knew it was wrong, but I couldn't help it, even after everything that had happened. The kitchen. Losing Octavia. I still couldn't get past the fact that Rube was my brother and that trouble was looming in his direction. I moved quickly back to our room, threw on my boots and spray jacket, and headed out.

It was close to eight when I got there, to the old train yard. I could see Rube waiting down by the fence, and I took a different street and a side alley. That way, I doubled back and stood closer, waiting. From near the edge of the alley, I could see him standing there, but he couldn't really see me. All I could do now was wait.

The yard was full of wrecked train carriages, standing around in the dark. Their windows were smashed, and stolen words were written across them like scars. The fence was tall and made of wire, cordoning off the yard from the street. Rube was leaning against it with his back.

For a moment, I wondered why he didn't bring friends, just in case. There were plenty of people around here who would gladly fight for him and could fight well. Maybe Rube decided this was his own doing and he would face it alone.

Thoughts passed.

Minutes passed.

Some voices started loitering around the street and soon their shadows turned into humans. There were three of them. I could see Rube straighten up as they went past me, not even noticing I was there.

They moved closer and adrenaline shot me down.

This was it.

DEEP BREATHS

My breath is made of smoke.

It crouches down.

Right after it comes from my mouth.

It crouches down, holds a moment, and is swallowed by the air.

I stand in the darkness, in the perpetual shadow. My eyes feel like they glow. My furry, furious hair knots upward for the stars. Thoughts scratch me. My life itches me, and I prepare.

To step out.

To rip the shadows from the ground and hoist the darkness from the air.

I look at my hands, my feet.

Deep breaths.

Breathe depths.

Solemnly, I nod, to myself.

Make a step.

Take a threat.

Not far away, there's one last fight, one last struggle.

There's something here, in this place — a smell. It's all that's awful, all that's precious, raw and real.

When I walk out and face it, I notice what it is.

This place smells.

Like brothers.

18

I waited for the sound of it.

The jabs of words and the left hook of the fight's beginning.

But nothing came.

The footsteps of the three figures turned into another small alley, and again, Rube was alone down at the fence. He leaned backwards again, moving back and forth into the wire.

He's late, I could see him thinking. He looked at his wrist, even though he never wears a watch.

By half-past eight I decided I should get going. As I moved away, I scuffed the ground and Rube looked up and saw me, or at least an edge of me.

'Oi!' he called, and he came towards me. I froze. 'What are y' doin' here, Cam?'

I shoved my hands in my pockets. 'I don't know.'

We met under a streetlight that poured over the street. It was the only light on.

'He's late,' my brother said. A long time elapsed before I answered.

'Maybe *we* should have it out instead.'

'What?'

'You heard me.'

Rube scanned the street for any more people but it was still deserted. He looked back at me and said, 'Have what out?'

'You and me and Octavia and the kitchen and Scraps – how's that for a start?' I said the words quickly, instantly.

'I don't have time for that tonight, Cam.'

'Fair enough,' and I started walking off. My feet scraped the road. 'When you and me are important enough, let me know.'

A fair way up the street, I heard him call out.

'Cameron!'

I turned. 'What?'

'Get back here.'

And I walked back to my brother and said it all. We stood under the streetlight that showered over us. My words were fists and I threw them at my brother. There was no hesitation. 'Why'd y' have to do it, Rube? Tell me. Why did you have to ruin my first chance – my first chance ever?' The combination of words lunged at my brother, hitting him in the face.

He took them well and came back. 'I don't know, OK!'

'Yes you do.'

The light seemed even brighter now. No place to hide.

'All right,' he said angrily, conceding. He looked at the ground, as though he were reading it, checking the sentences over before he said them. 'I just — bloody hell, Cam — I didn't want you to have her.'

'That's it?' I was incensed. 'Why the hell not!?'

'Because . . .' He shifted feet. 'You'd treat her so sickeningly bloody good, Cam, and I'd have to look at her as she compared us and thought about what a bastard *I* am, OK?' My brother's eyes sank into mine. 'That good enough for y'?'

I let the realization of that kick in. It took a while. Eventually, when I went to speak, Rube beat me to it. He said, 'I didn't know she'd get the hell out of there so fast either. How could I know that, Cam? . . . Do you think I haven't been walkin' round hating myself? Of course I have.'

We stood there.

Should I have pitied him, or hated him?

So long went by and finally, I realized it was me who had to break the silence. Everything was changing, on a quiet back street, with no one but ourselves to watch.

I said, 'You were always the one, Rube. You always got the girls.' I looked him flatly in the face. 'But not one of those girls ever got *you*. They got your filthy good looks, your hands, and everything else you wear, but they never got you. You're too busy taking to give anything . . .'

An even more penetrating silence arrived then, and I knew it was time to leave.

Rube remained a few paces away from me, shocked by what he'd heard, or actually, not that he'd heard it, but that someone else had told him exactly what he'd been trying to tell himself for a long time but refused to hear.

Just before I left, I said, 'You weren't only my brother, Rube – you were my best friend.'

He nodded then, and I could see emotion welling in his eyes.

'I'll see y' then.'

'Yeah,' he spoke quietly, 'I'll see y' later,' and I walked off. Not triumphant or successful. Just satisfied that what needed to be done was finished.

At the top of the street, I called back one last time.

'Y' comin' home?'

Rube shook his head. 'No, I'm waitin' a bit longer.'

With that, I turned back onto the street that belonged to the world – the one leading to the train yard seemed removed, like it was its own entity. As I walked, I imagined the shadow of Rube, still leaning against the fence, waiting. One of his feet would be up against the wire and his breath would be going smoky in the winter air.

When I made it home, I didn't do too much at all. I thought about our conversation and started reading a book for school. Not one word made it inside me.

The night went on and I resolved to wait up for Rube. I fell asleep on the couch a few times, and when everyone else went to bed they woke me and told me to go as well. I wanted to keep hating him, but as the hours went by, a strange determination kept growing inside. No matter how much I hated him, I was determined to see Rube come walking through the front door. Don't ask me why, but I needed to see it.

I wanted to see his face.

Unmarked.

Unbruised.

I wanted to hear his voice tell me to get up as he went past.

But that night, my brother Rube didn't come home.

It was just past midnight when I woke up with a silent start. My eyes opened and the yellow light from the lounge room sliced me through the eyes.

I was hit twice by one thought.

Rube.

Rube.

His name was repeated in me as I scissored off the couch and walked slowly into our room. I was hoping against hope that he would be in there, sprawled out across his bed. The darkness of the hall captured me. The creaking floorboards gave me away. Then, as the door crept open, I sent my eyes into the room, ahead of me. It was empty.

I turned the light on and shivered. It blinded me and I realized. I was going back out, to the night.

In the lounge room, I pulled my shoes on as quietly as possible, slipped my jacket back on, and headed for the kitchen, towards the front door. A pale light from the moon was numb in the sky. I was out in the uncertain coldness of the street.

A bad feeling intensified in my stomach.

It made its way to my throat.

Soon, as I walked fast to the old train yard, I could feel it gathering on its way through me. There were drunk people who made me edge out onto the road. Cars sped toward me with the brightness of their lights, then passed and faded away.

My hands sweated inside my jacket pockets. My feet were cold inside the warmth of my shoes.

'Hey, boy,' a voice slung out to me. I avoided it. I pushed past the guy who said it and broke into a run and had the street leading to the train yard in sight.

When I made it there, I could feel my heartbeat's hands, ripping me open.

The street.

Was empty.

It was empty and dark except for the widening light of the moon that seemed to spray down on each forgotten corner of the city. I could smell something. Fear.

I could taste it now.

It tasted like blood in my mouth, and I could feel it slide through me and open me up when I saw him . . .

There was a figure sitting down, crooked, against the fence.

Something told me Rube didn't sit like that.

I called his name, but I could barely hear it. There was a giant pounding in my ears that kept everything else out.

Again, I called, 'Rube!?'

The closer I got, the more I knew it was him. My brother was slumped against the fence and I could see the blood flooding his jacket, his jeans, and the front of his old flanno.

His hands gripped the fence.

The look on his face was something I'd never seen on him before.

I knew what it was because I was feeling it myself.

It was the fear.

It was fear, and Ruben Wolfe had never been afraid of anything or anyone in his life, until now. Now he was sitting alone in the city and I knew that one person alone couldn't have done this to him. I imagined them holding him down and taking turns. His face almost made its way into a smile when he saw me, and like a breeze through the silence, he said to me blankly:

'Hey, Cam. Thanks for comin'.'

The pulse in my ears subsided and I crouched down to my brother.

I could tell he'd dragged himself to this position on the fence. There was a small trail of blood smeared to a rusty colour on the cement. It looked like he'd climbed two metres when it was too much and he couldn't go on. I had never seen Ruben Wolfe defeated.

'Well' – he shuddered – 'I guess they got me good, huh? You must be glad . . .'

I ignored this comment. I had to get him home. He was shivering uncontrollably. 'Can you get up?'

He smiled again. 'Of course.'

Rube still had that smile perched on his lips when he staggered up the fence and collapsed. I caught him and held him up. He slipped through me and fell face-down, holding onto the road.

The city was swollen. The sky was still numb.

Ruben Wolfe was face-down on the road with his brother standing there, helpless and afraid, next to him.

'You've gotta help me, Cam,' he said. 'I can't move.' He pleaded with me. 'I can't move.'

I turned him over and saw the concussion that surrounded him. There wasn't as much blood as I'd originally though, but his face was brutalized by the night sky that fell on him and made him real.

I dragged him back to the fence, propped him up, and lifted him. Again, he nearly collapsed, and when we started walking, I knew he wasn't going to make it.

'I'm sorry, Cam,' he whispered. 'I'm sorry.'

'We'll just get y' home, ay.'

'No,' he said, hanging onto me. 'Not sorry for *this* – sorry for everything.' His expression swallowed me.

'OK,' I said. 'We're OK.'

That was when relief seemed to wash over him and he fell to the ground. Maybe that was the sweetest punch – and the final defeat. 'We're OK, huh?' I had never heard a person so happy in this condition.

We'd travelled only about five metres from the fence.

I rested for a minute as my brother continued lying on his back . . .

As the moon was smothered by a cloud, I slid my arms beneath my brother's back and legs and picked him up. I was holding Rube in my arms and carried him up the deserted street.

On the way home, my arms ached and I think Rube fell unconscious, but I couldn't rest. I couldn't put him down. I had to make it home.

People watched us.

Rube's tough curly hair hung down towards the ground.

Some extra blood landed on the footpath. It dripped from Rube onto me and then onto the path.

It was Rube's blood.

It was my blood.

Wolfes' blood.

There was a hurt somewhere far down inside me, but I walked on. I had to. I knew that if I stopped carrying him it would be harder to keep going.

'Is he all right?' a young party-going sort of guy asked. I could only nod and continue walking. I wouldn't stop until Rube was in his bed and I was standing over him, protecting him from the night, and from the dreams that would wake him in the hours until morning.

The last turn into our street finally came and I lifted him in one last effort.

He moaned.

'Come on, Rube,' I said. 'We're gonna make it,' and when I think about it now, I don't understand how I made it that far. He was my brother. Yes, that was it. He was my brother.

At our gate, I used one of Rube's feet to free the latch and walked up the porch steps.

'The door,' I said, louder than I'd wanted to, and after putting him down on the porch, I opened the flyscreen, got my key in, and turned back to face him. My brother. *My brother Rube*, I thought, and my eyes ached.

As I walked back towards him, my arms throbbed and my spine climbed my back. When I picked him up again, we nearly fell together into the wall.

On the way through the house, I managed to jam one of Rube's knees into a door frame, and by the time I got us into our room, Sarah was standing there, sleepy-eyed until terror strangled her face.

'What the hell—'

'Quiet,' I said. 'Just help me.'

She stripped the blanket off Rube's bed and I placed him down on it. My arms were on fire as I took his jacket and flanno off, leaving him in his jeans and boots.

He was cut up and badly bruised. A few ribs were swollen and one of his eyes was pitch-black. Even his knuckles were bleeding. *He got a few good ones in,*

I thought, but all of that meant nothing now.

We stood there. Sarah looked from Rube to me, recognizing his blood on the arms of my jacket. She cried.

The light was off now but the hall light was on.

We could feel someone else arrive and I knew it was Mrs Wolfe. Without even looking, I could picture the hurt expression on her face.

'He'll be OK,' I managed to say, but she didn't leave. She came towards us as Rube's voice fought its way next to me.

His hand came out from under the blanket and held onto mine.

'Thanks,' he said. 'Thanks, brother.'

The pale light hit me from the window. My heart howled.

THE EYES HAVE IT

I see myself standing on a city street, where a flood of people crowds towards me. Somehow, I manage to stay still, and I soon realize that all of these people are faceless. A blankness shrouds their eyes and they have no expression at all.

It's only when I begin to walk, through the gaps, against

the flow, that I notice that some of the faces have actually kept their form.

At one point, I see Sarah, finding her own way through, and at another, I see my father, and Mrs Wolfe, walking together, holding hands.

A long way off, I see Octavia.

I don't see her face, because she's going in the same direction as me. I see only her hair, and her neck and shoulders through the crowd.

Of course, like before, my first instinct is to go after her – but immediately, I stop. I stop and look to my right and see my reflection, even though there's no mirror or glass to speak of. There's only a concrete wall, but I'm able to see myself.

I see my eyes.

They're eyes of hunger and desire.

They tell me:

Don't move from here – not yet.

They ask me:

Are you OK, Cameron?

I think about it and take a good look at me. I look at my boyish arms, my dirty fingers and wanting face. I look at the eyes, and I see the hunger and desire, growing and feeding, determined to make me worthwhile, to be somebody on my own.

And I nod.

I can move on now, because here, at this moment, no matter how fragile it might be, I can feel OK-ness growing inside me.

The funny thing is that OK-ness is not a real word. It's not in the dictionary.

But it's in me.

19

I'll give it to him.

Rube actually got up the next morning and went to work with Dad and me. He was bruised and still prone to constant bleeding, but he still showed up and worked as hard as he could. I don't think there are many people who could take a beating like that and get up the next day and work.

That was Rube.

There isn't anything else I can say to explain it.

Everyone woke up in the morning when he and Dad argued, but once it was over, that was it. Mrs Wolfe asked, or actually, begged Rube to stay in at night more often, and there was no way he'd be arguing with that. He agreed completely and we filed out to the car and left. In the car, I could smell him – there was disinfectant on all his cuts.

It was mid-afternoon when Rube finally asked about some of the hazier details of the previous night.

'So how far was it, Cam?' His words came

and stood in front of me. They wanted the truth.

I stopped work. 'How far what?'

'You know.' He caught himself in my eyes. 'How far did you carry me last night?'

'A fair way.'

'All the way?'

I nodded.

'I'm sorry,' he went to say, but we both knew it wasn't needed.

'Forget about it,' I said.

The rest of the afternoon passed by pretty quickly. I watched Rube work at times and knew that somehow he'd be all right. He was just that type. If he was alive, he'd be all right.

'What are y' lookin' at?' he asked me later, when he saw me watching him and wondering about it.

'Nothin'.'

We even afforded a laugh, especially me, because I decided I had to stop being caught when I was watching people. Watching people isn't really a bad habit in my opinion. It's the getting caught I need to cut out.

When we got home, there was a present waiting for me, on my desk in Rube's and my room. It was an old grey typewriter with black keys. I stopped and looked at it from a few steps away.

'You like it?' came a voice from behind. 'I saw it in a secondhand shop and had to buy it.' She smiled and touched the back of my arm. 'It's yours, Cam.'

I walked to it and touched it. My fingers ran along the keys and I felt it under me.

'Thank you.' I turned round and faced her. 'Thanks, Sarah. It's beautiful.'

Later on, Sarah was on the phone for a while, talking to Steve. His semifinal was on the next day and everyone decided on going. What I didn't count on was Steve coming down to our place later that night.

I was on the front porch when his car pulled up and he walked towards me. He stood there.

'Hi, Cam.'

'Hi, Steve.'

I stood up and we both watched each other. I remembered the last time we'd spoken down here. Tonight, though, Steve's face was shattered, like it was at the oval, way back at the start of winter.

'I heard what happened last night,' he began. 'Sarah told me on the phone.'

'You came to see Rube?' I asked. 'He's in bed, but

I'd say he's still awake.' I went to open the door, but Steve didn't go in.

He stayed in front of me and didn't move.

'What?' I asked. 'What?'

His voice was abrupt, but quiet. 'I didn't come here to see Rube – I came to see you.' He adjusted his eyes slightly. More respectful. 'Sarah told me you carried him home from the old train yard . . .'

'It wasn't anything—'

'No. Don't lie, Cam. It *was* something.' He stood above me, but it was only a physical thing now. A matter of height. 'It was something, all right?'

I agreed with him. 'All right.'

Steve stood there.

I stood there.

The silence collected between us, and we smiled at each other.

He went inside a bit later but didn't stay long. He came and said goodbye not long after I went in to write on the typewriter. No words came.

In truth, I think the typewriter scared me, because I wanted to write perfectly on it. I was still staring at it just after ten o'clock.

Soon, I thought. *The words will come soon . . .*

The weeks travelled and winter was drawing to a

close. Steve won his grand final. Rube and I were brothers again, though things had changed now for ever. He healed up nicely and was still far too handsome for his own good. If anything, his scars would make him even more desirable.

Dad didn't need us at work too much, and one Saturday afternoon, I was curious about Octavia Ash. I still wanted her badly, and on many occasions I'd imagined us being together. I hoped she felt the same. There were no days or nights without her, and on the last Saturday of winter, I went down to the harbour to see if she was there. I hoped she was, mainly because I didn't want her to be still hiding from me. I wanted her to stay as she was, whether she wanted me or not. The harbour belonged to her, and I would have hated myself if I took that away from her.

I boarded a train at Central and made it in quick time to Circular Quay.

From the platform, I saw the people.

They were crowded around the girl with the harmonica, and a familiar feeling showed its face in me again. *Octavia Ash*, I thought, and I went down there, to watch from far away, and maybe hear just a few musical glimpses that came from her mouth. *One more chance*, I thought.

I caught a bus to Bronte in the afternoon and looked for another shell. I didn't find one like the first one. I didn't even try. The one I found was slightly broken, but it was beautiful nonetheless. It had soft ripples and a tanned colour that was worn into it. That night, I told Rube what I'd be doing with it the next day. He didn't object. In fact, I think he was glad. He wanted it.

'Y' don't mind?' I asked.

He shook his head. 'No – I'll even come with you if y' want.'

It didn't matter any more. There was no animosity. Not even any thought that Octavia and Rube had ever been together. That felt so long ago now. We were different people. Octavia never *had* been with Rube – not in *this* life. Not in the life that began the night I carried my brother home.

'So do you mind?' he asked again.

'What?'

'If I come with y'?'

I thought about it and it felt right.

'No worries,' I said.

The next day arrived and we caught the train. On the platform at Circular Quay, I took the shell from my pocket and we made our way down.

'Good luck,' said Rube. He stayed back and waited.

The crowd was there.

The girl was there, and today, I didn't hesitate.

I walked through the crowd and stood before her, then crouched down. When the music stopped, I kissed the shell and gently placed it in the jacket, stood back, and looked into her. 'I'm Cameron Wolfe,' I said. My eyes blurred but I kept talking. 'And I miss you . . .'

The words registered and for a moment, Octavia and I stood there, silent, along with the crowd.

'Well?' some old lady asked, just as I noticed that Octavia was still wearing the necklace she'd made out of the previous shell. Maybe there was some hope . . .

I wanted to hear her voice. I wanted her to say that she already had a shell like that but that she'd take it anyway. And I wanted to see her smile – the straight line of teeth that crowded at the edges.

None of that came, though.

We only stood.

'I'll wait by the water,' I spoke quietly. 'If you want to come over when you're finished, I'll be there. If not, it's all right,' and I walked away, back through the crowd. A silence stretched itself out until the music arrived like a knot. When I crouched at the water, I could still hear it, and I knew I'd done enough, whether she came to me later or not, I'd done enough.

I'd forgotten all about Rube, but it wasn't long until he was behind me.

'Cam?'

'Hey, Rube.'

'It went OK?'

'I think so.'

As he crouched down, his hands played with his pockets. We both stared at the water, and I could tell Rube was falling apart, just slightly. He looked on and said, 'I'll go in a second, but first I have to tell you somethin' . . .' He looked at me now. We were in each other's eyes.

'Rube?' I asked.

The water of the harbour rose up and dived down.

'See,' he said. 'All my life I sort of expected you to look up to me, y' know?' The expression on his face only just held on.

I nodded.

'But now I know,' he went on. 'Now I know.'

I waited but nothing came. I asked, 'Know what?'

He stared into me and his voice shook as he said, 'That I look up to you . . .'

His words circled me and went in. They got beneath my skin and I knew there was no way out. They were in there for always, and so was this moment, between Ruben Wolfe and me.

We crouched there, and when we finally stood up and turned to face the world, I could feel something climbing through me. I could feel it on its hands and knees inside me, rising up, rising up – and I smiled.

I smiled, thinking, *the hunger*, because I knew it all too well.

The hunger.

The desire.

Then, slowly, as we walked on, I felt the beauty of it, and I could taste it, like words inside my mouth.

THE EDGES OF WORDS

I sit here by the water, writing only in my mind.

At home, the typewriter waits.

At my side, a girl sits silently, and I'm thankful, because, in the end, I realize I didn't get this girl, in every way that means—

I found her.

And I want to keep finding her, for as long as we allow.

. . . The water looks at us, and I think now, of the edges of words, the loyalty of blood and the music of girls. I think of the hands of brothers, and of hungry dogs that howl through the night.

There are so many moments to remember, and sometimes I think that maybe we're not really people at all. Maybe moments are what we are.

Moments of weakness, of strength.

Moments of rescue, of everything.

I see people walking through the city and wonder where they've been, and what the moments of their lives have done to them. If they're anything like me, their moments have held them up and shot them down.

Sometimes I just survive.

But sometimes I stand on the rooftop of my existence, arms stretched out, begging for more.

That's when the stories show up in me.

They find me all the time.

They're made of footsteps not only to the girl, but to

me. *They're made of hunger and desire and trying to live decent.*

The only trouble is, I don't know which of those stories comes first.

Maybe they all just merge into one.

We'll see, I guess.

I'll let you know when I decide.

ABOUT THE AUTHOR

Markus Zusak is the author of five novels,
including the internationally bestselling
The Book Thief, which is translated into
over thirty languages.

He lives in Sydney with his wife and daughter.

Also available by

MARKUS ZUSAK

and published by Definitions

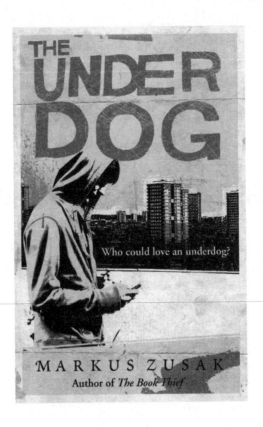

Cameron is hopeless, pitiful, and a shake-your head kind of pathetic. What he really wants is to meet a girl. But who could love an underdog like Cameron Wolfe?

The uplifting debut novel from the author of the international bestseller, *The Book Thief.*

The Wolfe brothers know how to fight. They've been fighting all their lives. Now there's something more at stake than just winning.

'An impressive and heartwarming story
of fraternal and familial bonding'
Irish Times

This is the tale of the book thief, as narrated by death.
And when death tells a story, you really have to listen.

'Extraordinary, resonant and relevant,
beautiful and angry'
Telegraph